That Night

THAT NIGHT

CYN BALOG

sourcebooks
fire

Published by Sourcebooks Fire, an imprint of Sourcebooks.
P.O. Box 4410, Naperville, Illinois 60567-4410
(630) 961-3900
Fax: (630) 961-2168
sourcebooks.com

Library of Congress Cataloging-in-Publication Data

Names: Balog, Cyn, author.
Title: That night / Cyn Balog.
Description: Naperville, Illinois : Sourcebooks Fire, [2019] | Summary: The more Hailey struggles to understand her boyfriend's apparent suicide, despite the discouragement of his stepbrother, her best friend, Kane, the more she remembers and the more secrets are revealed.
Identifiers: LCCN 2019000363 | (trade pbk. : alk. paper)
Subjects: | CYAC: Suicide--Fiction. | Secrets--Fiction. | Memory--Fiction. | Friendship--Fiction.
Classification: LCC PZ7.B2138 Th 2019 | DDC [Fic]--dc23 LC record available at https://lccn.loc.gov/2019000363

Printed and bound in the United States of America.
VP 10 9 8 7 6 5 4 3 2 1

For all the beautiful fools.

No amount of fire or freshness can
challenge what a man will store up
in his ghostly heart.

—*The Great Gatsby*, F. Scott Fitzgerald

Now

It didn't end with you blowing your head off in the back shed behind your house.

It didn't end with your funeral, where we stood without umbrellas in a driving rain that couldn't disguise our pain.

It didn't end after my resulting spiral into depression, or my six-month stay at Shady Harbor, or the thousands of hours of therapy I endured.

It didn't even end with your mom going through your stuff a year later to make room for the new baby—the replacement Weeks child.

Maybe that was when it started. With what your mom found.

I thought being the girlfriend of a boy who'd blown his head off was rock bottom. I thought I'd been through hell.

But I can't come out of this. Hell isn't a hallway between two better places. It is a chasm, so deep and wide that the more I try to pull myself out, the farther I fall in.

There is no way I'll ever get out.

The best I can do is try to make myself comfortable.

754 Days Before

Kane Weeks likes to be first at everything.

He was the first kid to learn to tie his shoes in kindergarten. The first of us to use the f-word, the first to get drunk, the first to own a cell phone.

So it was only natural that he was the first to have sex.

It was years ago, and *that* eventful. Everyone knew about it. I know, because I was the one he had sex with.

Kane's had a long line of girls since then. But it's hard for me to forget, since he's it. The one. The only. The end.

I was *his* first too. We were fifteen, too cool to play in all the snow that had graced us with a glorious three-day weekend. Instead, we sat cross-legged on the shag carpet in Kane's room, playing some zombie video game. I kept losing. After my brains were eaten for the hundredth time, I threw down my controller and shouted obscenities at the television, then turned to him, about to ask what we should do next.

As usual, he read my mind. He quirked a quarter smile at me and drew out a mischievous "So…"

That one word, coming out of Kane's mouth, always means trouble. His blue eyes turned stormy, and his hair fell into his face in a way that recently made my heart flutter. I hated that flutter, hated that the charm I'd been immune to all my life suddenly had an effect on me. At fifteen, he'd never had a gangly or awkward day in his life. He said, "Don't you ever wonder what it's like? What all the talk is about?"

"Um. What are we talking about?"

"You know," he whispered, checking the door. "*It.*"

Oh. *It* it. *It* consumed everyone at the school like the plague. Everyone spoke about it, whispered about it, joked about it. You couldn't avoid the subject, but I did my best. In a lot of ways, it was even scarier to me than that clown in Stephen King's *It*.

But nothing scared Kane.

"Sometimes," I said. I did wonder, vaguely. Mostly I fantasized about having my first kiss with some debonair Prince Charming, and occasionally my mind would stray past that to things I'd only seen in movies. But Kane was used to kissing. He'd had girlfriends since fifth grade.

"So let's do it," he said.

I didn't *always* blindly follow Kane Weeks. But he was my best friend. We didn't have to swear blood oaths or cross our hearts; we trusted each other, the way you'd trust that your welcome mat would be under your feet the second you stepped to your front door. Whatever he was saying, I was usually thinking. We'd played doctor when we were kids, him groping under my shirt and making me giggle because I knew it wasn't right but it didn't feel all that wrong either. So I agreed.

"Here?" I asked.

"Yeah."

Not that we would have gone anywhere else. The tension in my home suffocated me. His house was the only place we ever hung out. The door to his bedroom was closed. Even so, I could hear his dad down the hall, rattling the keys on the laptop in his office. His dad rarely left that office. Dishes piled up in a fortress around his desk, the smell of stale oatmeal and rotting fruit sometimes wafting down the hall. But Kane's room was like a trophy showroom—dozens of little gold figures wielding baseball bats stared down at us, our only audience.

Kane untied his sweatpants. I undid the zipper on my jeans and pulled them off, hiding my panties in them as I neatly folded my pants at the foot of his bed.

"Now what?" I asked. I looked at his penis and started to get scared because I'd never seen one that didn't include arrows pointing out the scrotum, the sperm duct, and other anatomical parts I couldn't quite remember. He was looking at me too, at everything I didn't have. Not in a lustful way, like in movies—he craned his neck and cocked his head to the side with scientific curiosity.

He told me to lie down, so I did. He climbed on top of me and told me to spread my legs. He weighed a ton. Suddenly, his body was so much more than a picture in a textbook. It was between my thighs, poking me. I had to stifle a giggle. I was pretty sure that while it was okay when I was seven and we were playing doctor, giggling wasn't appropriate now. Having his skin against mine was no big deal because we were close, but he'd never been *there* before. "Is that the right place?"

"Um," I managed. The right place for what? "I don't know."

"Geez, Hail. Haven't you ever watched porn?"

"No," I mumbled. *Had he?* He probed and prodded against me, and I finally had to tell him I didn't think he was in the right place after all. Frustrated, he moved his hand between us and guided himself closer, his eyes never meeting mine. He pushed again. This time, he got it right. It didn't hurt. He sank into me like a hypodermic needle without the pinch, like the tampons I'd started using earlier that summer. Then he stayed there, bearing down on me for the longest time, until his heartbeat and the clattering of laptop keys all mingled together and I imagined being so flattened like Silly Putty that he'd have to peel me off his sheets later. The sweat coming through his T-shirt soaked my stomach.

"Oh shit," he'd said before I could ask him what was supposed to happen next. More doubt crept in. I'd helped Kane on many of his adventures—trying to sail his raft in the retention pond out back, making barbeque-sauce-flavored ice cream, holiday caroling to make money for a trip to Disney (we made $3.50, and most of that was from our own parents)—but this was certainly one of our stupider ones. He pulled off me, looked down at his sheets, and grimaced. "Whoa."

I could've asked him to kiss me. He would've, maybe, because I never asked for much. But for some reason, that seemed scarier than what we had just done. I knew his mouth much better than the part of his body that had been inside me. Those parts we could hide afterward—forever, if we chose. Go on with our regularly scheduled lives and pretend it had never happened between us. But as I scooted up to the headboard and reached out for my pants, I realized how backward it had been. I'd never had a real kiss, but I'd had sex.

But this was what everyone was talking about. I figured that if sex was *that*, then kissing probably sucked hardcore.

"Is that all it was?" I'd said to him breezily when he sat on the side of the bed and leaned over to retrieve his underwear. "Hardly seems worth the buzz."

We never talked about it after that. It was like a footnote, something that I could almost believe hadn't happened. After that, he went back to having a steady stream of girlfriends, so I guess it *was* worth the buzz, considering the way they lined up for him, and the way he never turned them down.

But to me, he was just Kane—nothing and everything at once.

Present Day:
Thursday, February 14

I've lost a lot of memories, but not that one.

That day—that seemingly stupid, insignificant day—hadn't only settled in my mind. It oozed around every cell inside my head like glue, taking up all available space. Even now, I can't think of another memory without that one shading it. Though so much has happened in between, it's like I'm right back there again in his bed when we were fifteen. As I lean against the door of my Jeep, watching Kane say goodbye to some of his admirers, I'm doing it again, trying to pick that thought out of my brain.

Damn him.

Kane Weeks doesn't have to lift a finger to be a magnet to the opposite sex. He has female admirers coming out his ears, more girls than he knows what to do with.

"Please tell me those aren't all yours," I mumble as he saunters up to me holding a cardboard shoebox filled with flowers.

"They are," he says, smiling down at them. "I only sent one, though."

"Stupidly." I pull the sleeves of my oversize sweatshirt down and hook my thumbs through the holes I'd ripped in the seams of the cuffs.

He ignores my comment. "You got it, right?"

"I did. Homeroom. Thanks." I try to sound sincere, but I didn't want a dumb pity flower. From him, from anyone.

Every February, the Key Club sells carnations, which are delivered to students throughout the day on Valentine's Day. It's never mattered to me in the least, but there are always rumors about girls giving blow jobs to win the honor of receiving the most.

The male winner is no contest. It's yet another talent that comes effortlessly to Kane. He inspects his fingernails nonchalantly as he waits for me to pop the locks. I watch him secure the lid and toss the box into the back seat of my Jeep as if it's his gym bag.

That's the most perplexing thing. He doesn't even care about the attention.

"You like what it said?" he asks.

I nod as I squeeze into the driver's seat, cranking the heat to ward off the frigid 20-degree air. *Happy Day of Suck*, it'd said.

Valentine's Day. This time last year, it'd been snowing. We'd huddled together in the backyard of his house, his arms around me, and I'd cried so hard that I couldn't breathe. That was the last time Kane touched me.

"I was going to text you, but I forgot about your technological deficiency," he says. "When are you going to remedy that situation?"

I haven't had a phone in nearly a year, ever since I smashed mine. Not that I care. Other people seem to miss me having it more than I do. "Never," I reply.

He scowls. "Your parents?"

"No. Me. I don't want one."

"Weirdo."

I know. That's actually being kind. I shrug.

I drive him the three miles to our neighborhood as he uses the glove compartment, the center console, his thighs, my head to pretend to play the drum solo to the music on his iPhone. No one would ever accuse my red Wrangler that's just shy of two hundred thousand miles of being a smooth ride. When I got it the August after my sixteenth birthday, Declan called it my Pretty Piece of Crap. He'd managed to fix it up to run, but it's been withering from his lack of attention, so it has trouble doing even that now. Every one of its parts rattles, and the wind blows steadily through the Swiss-cheese soft top. Kane has to yell to talk to me when I drive, so we don't talk much.

I don't mind that. I don't mind the noise either. It helps me avoid thinking too much. I don't want to think too much. Not today.

He yells over the roar of the engine to tell me that he won't need a ride for the rest of the week. Baseball is beginning soon, and he needs to start lifting again to get in shape. Last spring, he made Varsity All-Stars. Somehow he was able to get right back into the swing of sports and after-school activities. Unlike me. His college application shines. Unlike mine.

We live in a gated community, which might sound fancy, but it's not. Our houses make up half of the homes on the Fox Court cul-de-sac. The homes are tall and thin and right on top of each other, so they remind me of dominoes. Kane's house is almost a mirror image of mine. When Declan and his mom moved in three years ago, the Mayflower truck got stuck in the throat of the roundabout. Thank God for trees, Declan once said, or we'd all know each other's business.

Kane texts Luisa as I downshift and cruise into the court. "She's insane, you know. How've you guys been friends this long?"

He has to know that we're not friends anymore. I haven't been friend material for anyone except the cocoon of my bed for a long time. I haven't been a lot of things I used to be. "What are you talking about? You're the one who's been going out with her for years."

"Not consistently. I can only take her in small doses."

That's Kane. Most people annoy him. I'm the only one who knows this. On the surface, he's this happy-go-lucky guy who loves everyone. Underneath? He has this dark, glass-half-empty, biting sarcasm. That bitterness is one of the reasons I can still tolerate him. I don't need anyone telling me, "Today is the first day of the rest of your life!" or "Time heals all wounds." When we get together, which is rare these days, we grumble. We complain like two old men who were denied their free senior coffee at McDonald's. "So what's bugging you about her currently?"

"Everything. She had an attitude today."

I scratch the side of my head and pretend to think. "Gee. Maybe it's because you sent *me* a flower instead of her?"

He shakes his head like that can't be it. "I only had two bucks. And I explained how it was to her."

I cringe. *How it was* makes it seem like I'm some bald, three-legged cat he decided to adopt from the animal shelter. Like I need Kane to take care of me. I'm fine. I'm just peachy—until people start asking me how I'm doing, not in a casual, *what's up* way, but in a lingering, *oh you poor thing* way. Whenever I answer "fine," they always seem suspicious, as though they want me to have a nervous breakdown at their feet.

My eyes trail to Kane's backyard. They removed the shed months ago, but there's still a stark brown rectangle of dirt. A giant scar. So, so ugly and sad.

So unlike the Declan I knew.

I shiver, recalling the day the world tilted. The day everything got a little brighter, more intense. The day I met him.

"You okay, Hail?" Kane asks me.

I'm gripping the steering wheel so hard that my knuckles are white. I loosen my hands. "Yeah. I hope you're doing something nice for that girlfriend of yours. Girls expect that."

He frowns. "You don't."

I give him a smile and bat my eyelashes. "I'm not a girl. I'm a woman."

He laughs like it's the most hilarious joke in the world. Like he wasn't the one who made me that way, if it can be said that sex makes a girl a woman. Which honestly is a crap thing to say, since it didn't make me feel any different and it gives him way too much credit. He took my virginity, not my freaking soul. "Whatever. Today is just another day."

He's only saying that for my benefit. It's not a day of suck because I have no one to share it with. I've never shared Valentine's Day with anyone, ever, and I've survived.

Before, it was simply another day.

Now, it's the anniversary of the worst day of our lives.

If that isn't the definition of a day of suck, I don't know what is.

I climb out of the Jeep, and Kane comes around to the driver's side, standing there as if he wants to say something. When we were fifteen, he was about my height. Now, he's a solid nine inches taller than me, and I hold my own at 5′6″. It's a good thing he's this tall, because from down here, it's easier to avoid his eyes. I look at the scuffed toes of my black Converse high tops and tell him I'll see him later.

Halfway up the drive to my house, Kane's stepmom calls to me.

I've talked to Mrs. Weeks about a dozen times since our worlds collectively turned to crap. Funny, she used to be such a straight-laced, business-suit-wearing, un-Californian person. Since she left the West Coast, though, she's become about as California hippie as you can imagine, with wild blond hair and a soft, faraway voice that makes you think she's been sucking on some really strong weed. The only feature she shares with her son is the arched, expressive shape of their eyebrows, though his were black as tar and hers are the color of honey.

But it's enough. Enough to make me see his face in hers, *every single time.*

It's both sad and pathetic that something as innocuous as an eyebrow tears me apart.

She waddles down the drive toward me, the bottom of her amorphous maxi skirt dusting the asphalt, her expanding belly poking out the front of her cardigan. I break into a run, because she looks like she's about to give birth on the sidewalk. When I get across the street, I notice the bulging black garbage bags on the porch. "We're getting ready to paint the nursery," she huffs out.

The nursery, a.k.a. no-man's-land. Hell of a time to clean out Declan's room. But she's said before that keeping busy helps her cope. In the past eight months, she's remodeled the house from top to bottom.

All except for one room.

Since I've gotten out of the hospital, that room has had its door closed every time I've stopped by. It's at the end of the hall and is visible from the foyer, right when you walk inside. Inescapable.

Mrs. Weeks told me, months ago, that I could take anything I wanted, anytime I wanted.

I didn't want.

I take a breath.

I fasten my eyes on a patch of gray snow on the sidewalk as she hands me a large Yuengling beer box. "I know you'd like to keep these things." Wrong. "But come on up and see what else."

"Actually, this is good." I hold the box like it's toxic waste. I don't want to go in his room. I imagine it smells like him, like soap and woodworker's glue and motor oil. Even this box does. Or maybe that's my imagination.

She looks over her shoulder as Kane helps lug the bag to the curb. She calls out, "Kane, there are a few more upstairs, for Goodwill."

"On it," he says, jogging inside.

She lowers her voice for me. "I wanted to get you alone, because I have to ask you something."

She starts unfolding an envelope. I already know it's something I don't want to see, like that brown scar in the backyard. Instinctively, I step back.

"Do you know what this is?"

She pulls a tiny photograph out of the envelope, the kind from one of those instant cameras. My gaze catches on it, and I can't look away.

It's like one of those kids' puzzles where objects are magnified to such an extent you can't really tell what they are. Body parts melding. Hair. Light and dark, smooth and textured, some shadowed, some overexposed. Skin upon skin. Declan's skin. My skin? And in the white space underneath, printed with a Sharpie in harsh block letters, the words:

THIS ENDS HERE.

583 Days Before

Bitch, bitch, bitch. Kane bitched like crazy sometimes.

This time, though, I had to admit he had a good reason.

His mother had been out of the picture for twelve years, and it'd been Kane and his dad ever since, living in that three-bedroom bachelor pad like a couple of fraternity brothers. His father was neater than the average frat guy, sure, but the absence of a woman's touch was obvious—Penn State curtains in the living room, where the only decor on the wall was a fifty-six-inch television set. The place always smelled like nachos, and there was never anything but beer and ketchup in the fridge. His father kept an antique carburetor from an old Mustang on the kitchen island because he thought it made a good centerpiece. Stuff like that.

Earlier that summer, Kane's dad had gone to SoCal on what we all thought was a business trip. Kane was pissed because he'd had to go to his aunt's house in Union for a whole week and miss out on baseball camp. I'd spent the entire week missing him. Luisa summered in Europe, so without either of them around, I was alone. Though things had been different in the months after we had sex. I'm not sure how. He didn't exactly avoid me, but something shifted. I tried to pretend like everything was the same. But I couldn't look at him without feeling him between my legs, closer to me than anyone could possibly get.

Funny, that thing I'd said was not worth all the fuss? As forgettable as it was, I couldn't stop thinking about it. Why had we done it? Wasn't it supposed to be about love? I did love Kane, in the pervasive, unmindful way that you love your own hands. I knew life would be shit without him. But maybe that wasn't love. Maybe that was dependence.

It was a humid day, one that makes everything stick together with sweat and everyone grumble. When my father drove me home from day camp at the local Y, he was harrumphing about how my mother hadn't picked up his dry cleaning before they closed that day. We both just wanted to get home, but we couldn't pull into the cul-de-sac because a huge moving truck was parked in the narrow opening, which made him mutter more. He ended up driving over the curb in his frustration, and I could see Kane sitting on his front porch steps, bouncing a ball and looking miserable in the way he would when he was alone and didn't have to put on his charming airs. I rushed across to see what was going on.

When I got there, Kane said, "He got married."

I was stunned. "Who?" popped out of my mouth before I could train my lips how to respond.

"Donald Trump. Who do you think? My dad. It wasn't a business trip. He went there to meet her, and then they got hitched in Vegas on the way here."

My mouth gaped. Kane's dad wasn't what you'd call a free spirit. He was a quiet, background IT guy prone to tinkering. The type of person you'd expect to carry an assortment of extra computer parts and cables on his person at all times. Steady, not one to do anything worthy of gossip. "Wow."

Kane mumbled under his breath and stood up. "Come on. I'll introduce you."

He threw the ball so hard against the pavement that it bounced over our heads but didn't touch ground again. It must have rolled up onto the roof and into the gutter. He cursed some more. I was beginning to understand his rage. His dad had gone on vacation without him, which would be enough to get me riled. But *bringing home a new mom*? I'd probably never speak to my dad again.

I thought Kane was bringing me inside to meet the new wife, which I didn't really want to do, but supposed it was polite. I followed him inside, doing what I usually did around him those days: trying my damnedest to force away the memory of that day in January. He brought me upstairs and stopped at the third bedroom at the end of the hall, which is my bedroom in my house, but in Kane's house had always been his dad's office. The door was open. Someone was strumming a guitar.

I looked at the person holding the guitar, and my heart stopped.

Everything stopped. I couldn't move in, out, anywhere.

He took his time raising his eyes to me. Time seemed to be slowing down. I'd find out later that was the Declan Effect. He prided himself on doing everything carefully, slowly—on being the tortoise while everyone else was trying to be the hare. He wore thick-rimmed, geeky glasses. He had on a white T-shirt under a loose bowling shirt, the colors contrasting nicely with his deep brown skin. Tight blue jeans. White socks and sneakers. All those things that, packaged together, you'd think would be quite goofy, and yet…it was hipster cool. No kid at our school dressed like that. They were all lemmings, too afraid to stand out. But this kid had style; he had a personality. I knew that much, and he hadn't even opened his mouth.

Me? I couldn't close *my* gulpy fish mouth.

"Hi," he said first.

Kane leaned against the door. "This is Hailey Ward. She lives across the street."

"Hailey, like the comet?" he asked.

My mouth had done half the work by opening, but words failed me.

Then he started to strum his guitar. He looked up at me and sang in a strong voice—something about a girl wearing a dress, her hair done up so nice. My hair was falling in my face. It was not done up nice at all. No dress, either. I'd come from Lazy Dazy Camp, where I'd spent eight hours teaching second-graders how to make bottle-cap ornaments in the hot sun. I was sweaty and probably smelled bad.

When he sang about my heart being cold as ice, I realized it wasn't an original work. Then he hit the guitar and broke into the chorus, which I'd heard before. "Shake, Rattle, and Roll." He stopped and grinned, and that's when I figured out who he looked like: one of those old-time dudes from the early days of rock 'n' roll. It was like he was caught in the fifties.

"Buddy Holly?" I murmured, not really sure, but I'd seen a movie on him. I think he died in a plane crash at the end.

"Bill Haley and the Comets," he said, breaking into another song, one I'd never heard before.

Oh. Who? I looked at Kane, who gave me a look like *Pity me because I have to live with him.* "So yeah. This is Declan. My..."

The kid stopped strumming and pulled the guitar strap over his head. "Stepbro. Right, man?" He held out his hand, palm up, but Kane just stared at it.

I said, almost too eagerly, "I'll give you some skin," and I did. I trailed my hand over his, light enough so we were barely touching.

His hand snapped, and he made like he was shooting me with his pointer finger. "All right," he said. His voice was so smooth, but not oily. Low already, seamless, like a man's. Nice. "My girl."

His girl? I had to giggle. Kane scowled at me.

I made an attempt to dig my hands into the pockets of my jean shorts but stopped after the third try. I was wearing sports shorts, without pockets. Declan noticed, because this amused smile crossed his face and his brown eyes danced. I pushed a lock of stray hair back to my ponytail. "Where are you from?"

"San Diego."

I looked over at Kane, reading his thoughts. We called California *The Land of Nuts and Honey*. I could hear his voice in my head. Declan wasn't looking at him, so Kane mouthed, *Nut*, and pantomimed *crazy* by twirling his finger by the side of his head.

"Are you…going to school with us in the fall?"

Declan studied me with these dark, almond-shaped eyes that were unlike anything I'd ever seen before. My face flamed. "Depends. What grade are you?"

"Tenth."

"Then nope," he said. "I'm going to be a junior. From what I hear, your high school is split into two. I'll be in the senior building."

He was right. Because of overcrowding, the district had to split us into two buildings that were, essentially, on the same campus but separated by a football field.

23

"Oh." Not only was Declan Kane's brother, but he was older. *First.* And Declan looked comfortable, even surrounded by cardboard boxes in his brand-new bedroom. No wonder Kane seemed like he wanted to punch him.

Instead, Kane grabbed my sleeve. "Come on."

I didn't want to. But I followed Kane, new feelings bubbling inside me. As I left, the kid started playing his guitar again, this time singing, "See you later, alligator..."

When we went downstairs, we sat in the gazebo at the back of his house. I sucked in humid air as if it were laced with a drug, feeling dazed, as if the world had shifted once again. Kane noticed and said, "What?"

I started to get defensive until I put together what was pissing him off. I had a grin plastered on my face, a goofy one. My cheeks were sore, probably because I'd never used those muscles that way for that long. I quickly wiped off the grin and said, "Wow. I can't believe your dad... I mean...he didn't even tell you?"

"Nope," he said, digging at a knot in the wood of the bench with his thumbnail. He trembled like a time bomb ready to go off. "It was supposed to be a visit, but they hit it off so well, they just went with it. You know California people. They're all free-spirited hippie types. They live for shit like this. How'd you know how to do that, anyway?"

"Uh. What?"

He seemed annoyed at me. "The skin thing?"

"Oh. I don't know. I think I saw it in a movie," I answered, still feeling tingly from where Declan's and my skin had almost touched. My goofy smile threatened to return, so I squelched it. "But your dad is…"

"Insane. Obviously." Kane stood up. "I've got to go. My dad wants to take us out to a family dinner. Some family."

Thursday, February 14

JUST BEFORE MIDNIGHT

I can't eat unless I'm under a blanket.

I've always been weird about food, but it's been a year since I stopped eating meals at the dinner table, in the cafeteria, or any place you'd normally eat food. It's been ten months since Juliet, my therapist, told my parents to let me. She said that they should allow anything that helps with the healing process, as long as it doesn't hurt me.

I'm not sure scarfing down Cheez-Its while under the covers of my bed is helping the healing. Still, I do it every night. Sometimes an entire box will disappear while I'm getting ready for bed.

I've slept with covers over my head since I was a little kid. My mother hated it because she was afraid I'd be smothered in my sleep. But I like being insulated from the world like this. Safe.

It's only since I got back from Shady Harbor that I've been inviting the Cheez-Its to accompany me.

My sheets are gritty with electric-orange crumbs. I smell and feel the sour cheddar and chemicals, and most mornings, my stomach hurts. I'm chubbier now, a side effect of the antidepressants. Or maybe I should say *pleasantly plump. Chubbier* implies that I care. And I really don't. Though Juliet says exercise would do me good, she agrees my improved mental state is more important than gaining a few extra pounds.

Not that my mental state is anything to cheer about.

I support the flashlight under my chin and shove another handful of cheddary goodness in my mouth as I turn the pages of a scrapbook I'd put together to give Declan last year. I never could take a good photo with my phone to save my life, but he was a master of selfies. He'd take them and text them to me, so after he died, I had more than a thousand of them.

Hence, smashing my phone. My parents packed me off to Shady Brook after that, before I could turn my wrath on the scrapbook.

I lean forward, squinting. In every shot, he has that same enormous smile. We're usually hugging tight, cheeks smushed together for the camera. Declan was a hugger. Unlike Kane, he was always touching me, and in all the best ways, making my spine dance and tingle, my every nerve bend toward him.

I've been through the Book of a Thousand Selfies so many times, and though every picture is essentially the same, I can tell you where each one was taken. I have my favorites, like the one taken after the giant slingshot ride at the shore. Or the one in front of home base at the Phillies game.

But God, that smile. You could harness its power and light all of Jersey with it for a year. It wasn't a sly, mischievous one like Kane's. Imagine a five-year-old boy's smile after catching his first fish on the Seaside pier. *That* was Declan's smile. Declan was never up to no good.

At least...

I shake crumbs off my T-shirt and unfold the envelope Mrs. Weeks gave me earlier. I turn the tiny photo around, adjusting the flashlight to illuminate the parts of it I want to study, but it doesn't become clearer. The light skin blurs with the dark, and the image is too pixelated and grainy to figure out. But something about one blotch looks familiar in color and shape.

My eyes burn from not blinking, so I squeeze them shut, then open them and try to refocus.

THIS ENDS HERE.

It's a threat.

I say the words over and over again, as the memories threaten to break through the dam and spill everywhere.

No.

Though Kane has the all-American looks, it was Declan who was the golden boy, the do-no-wrong kid who everyone would've hated if they didn't love him so much. Declan was a proud member of the geek club—he knew an unhealthy amount of information about Tolkien and Star Wars, and he rocked the astronomy club. In comparison, Kane never picked up a book, preferred sports, and raised a little hell. The Weeks boys might have been different in many ways, but they shared one attribute: charisma. It was hard not to love them.

I swallow, thinking of the funeral. Of all those cars lined up at the cemetery. Nearly everyone from school came. It was unseasonably warm. After all the snow we'd had that winter, no one had expected rain, so we all stood there, getting soaked without our umbrellas, dress shoes sinking into the patches of snow and mud. *Blessed are the dead that the rain falls on.*

I get why Mrs. Weeks was so perplexed by this picture. Declan was the last person anyone would want to threaten.

My eyes trail back to the Book of a Thousand Selfies, and I find something poking out from the pages. It's a dried carnation. Attached to it, a message in very familiar handwriting.

D—I love you, you amazing, wonderful,
gorgeous, but also completely insane person,
you. —H

I'd bought it for him last year. The only carnation I'd ever bought from the Key Club. I'd never written a love note before, never even said those words to another guy. But I didn't hesitate as I'd filled out the card. I knew he'd send me one too. He'd talked about it. He'd said I'd like the message, so I wasn't worried about rejection. Everything he did, everything he said, even the way he looked at me over those thick black frames of his, said *he loved me.*

I doubt so many things in my life. But I never doubted that. Not until…

My carnation for him sat in his homeroom the entire day, unclaimed. A hundred students probably walked by Mrs. Branson's desk and saw it there.

I'd texted him to see where he was. He never responded. I texted Kane, but Kane hadn't seen him either. There was a nasty flu going around. I figured he was down and out. Throughout the day, I kept feeling my face to see if it was hot, if I was coming down with the bug too.

We'd had early dismissal that day because of a threatening snowstorm. I claimed Declan's Valentine and came home in my Jeep, figuring I'd give it to him at home, along with some chicken soup and Nyquil.

It had started snowing. Mr. and Mrs. Weeks had just come home from the Poconos, where they'd gone for a long weekend. They were always doing things like that—acting like newlyweds, and leaving Declan and Kane at home on their own. Mr. Weeks went out to the shed in the back of the property to get more gasoline for his snow blower. The padlock on the barn door, which was usually secure, was hanging by the metal hinge.

He must have done it sometime during the day. Ironically, though no one remembers hearing the shot, we all heard his father's anguished wail. It was high-pitched and so, so sad.

We all raced through new snow to the backyard and found Mr. Weeks hunched over on his knees outside the shed, face buried in the heels of his hands. Kane tried to go inside, but Mr. Weeks lunged forward and grabbed him around the knees, begging him not to go in. Mrs. Weeks froze beside me, as if she was terrified to know what was in the shed.

My mind didn't process things right. All I could think, over and over again, was that no one would believe Declan killed himself. That smile wasn't only for selfies—it was Declan, all the time. He was always trying to pick me up out of the dumps. Hell, he rarely even frowned. The kid smiled in his sleep, for God's sake.

My mind hasn't been the same since. Thoughts float in and out at weird times and misshape themselves. Part of it is denial. Part of it is my stay at Shady Harbor. And part of it is just the good old passage of time.

Like, it wasn't until much, much later, while I was sitting in the art room at Shady Harbor, coloring a picture of a sunset, that it dawned on me that he hadn't sent me a Valentine. That thought floated into my head sometime in September. He'd said he would, told me he had it all written out, but still, *he hadn't.*

I pull the blanket off my head, and my long hair crackles with static. I shine the flashlight on the box Mrs. Weeks gave me, then cringe as I make out one of its components—a slender bud vase from Declan's junior prom. We'd made "us" official then, though we'd been dancing around the subject for months. Like I said, Declan took his time, which could be excruciating.

I already have a matching vase of my own that I buried in my closet to ward off the memories. I don't need his too.

I stand up, push the flaps of the box closed, and shove it under my bed. Then I climb under the covers, in a gritty but comforting sea of crumbs, and let the blankets fall on my face, breathing in the warm, stale air. My stomach is already revolting, but I savor the feeling. It's good to feel something, anything, because it means I'm still here.

Happy Suck Day.

524 Days Before

"You're the luckiest girl in school," Luisa said to me, throwing herself on my bed. "Sleeping this close to Kane Weeks every night."

I stuck out my tongue as though I wanted to vomit as I tried to apply eyeliner to my upper eyelid for the fortieth time.

"Are you crazy, Hail?" She threw a pillow at me. Good thing it missed, or I probably would've stabbed my eye with the pencil. "I mean, he's flawless. He must be some alien being, he's so perfect."

"He's not that perfect," I mumbled. "He has a birthmark."

Luisa got this professional cosmetics trunk for her fifteenth birthday, and it was filled with all these goodies. She'd been trying to give me a tutorial on making cat's eyes. The closest I'd achieved was a raccoon after a hard night of drinking. She rolled over to pick through the trunk and looked up. "No, he doesn't. Where?"

"On his butt or something. I saw it when we were kids," I said vaguely. I pulled away from the mirror and blinked. "How's this?"

She inspected my work and winced. "Uh…"

I swiped the wet washcloth off my dresser and swabbed at my eyes. "This is hopeless."

"Oh, no it's not," she said, batting her cat eyelashes at me and making me rue the day I ever thought I'd be able to do anything half as well as Luisa could. Luisa didn't need makeup, truthfully. We'd had countless sleepovers, and even after a night when we'd gotten a collective two hours of sleep, she'd wake up ready for a camera. She didn't get crud in the corners of her eyes or drool on her pillow like I did, and all she had to do was shake her head, and her blond hairs would fall dutifully into place. "So what's the stepbrother like?"

"His name is Declan. He's…kind of different."

She studied me. "Different, meaning hot?"

Well, yes, definitely—but I wasn't about to admit it. "Kane said that Declan's father was a mix of, like, six different ethnicities. Hawaiian, Japanese, and…I forget. He was an officer in the navy."

"Black?" she asked, surprised.

"Maybe. What difference does it make?"

"None. I mean, that's cool. I can't wait to meet him. I can't believe Kane's dad would just go off and do that," she said, shaking her head. "No wonder Kane is pissed."

"He told you?" I asked, confused. Sophomore year had only started a couple days earlier. I didn't think Kane had had any contact with anyone but me during the summer. I thought I was the one he complained to. The only one. The idea of him confiding in someone else made me a little queasy.

"No. It's hot gossip, though. Everyone knows." She'd slid into the glitter skirt I'd had to beg my mom for, since it was dangerously short, and a lace camisole that showed off the boobs she'd been growing. I couldn't wear that camisole unless I wore a shirt over it, because I had nothing to show off, but Luisa, as usual, showed me how my clothes were supposed to look. She whirled in front of the full-length mirror and said, "We should go over there."

I finished wiping my eyes. We'd been friends since kindergarten, but gradually, I'd been getting the feeling Luisa had just been putting up with me—that she had a much different reason for wanting to spend time at my house. After all, my house wasn't exactly a wonderland of fun. My parents circled each other like sharks, occasionally going in for bites, and I didn't have a big-screen TV or a pool or video games.

My house's one attribute was its proximity to Kane and Declan Weeks, and I guess that was enough.

"It's nearly eleven. What do you want to do? Pull a Romeo outside his window?"

She tapped her blood-red lips with her finger. "Maybe." Then she looked at herself in the mirror and said, "We look so hot. It's a shame to waste this."

Right. I was wearing my pajamas, and my eyes looked like I'd gone ten rounds in a prizefight. She'd done my lips nice, though, and put my hair up in this spunky, curly do on the top of my head. I grabbed my phone. "If you want to see them, I can text Kane."

"Oh my God, no!" she said, grabbing the phone from me. "That'd be desperate. Let's... I don't know. Walk around the court. Like we're minding our own business. *Please.*"

"All right."

So that was how we ended up parading ourselves around and around the cul-de-sac at not quite midnight on a Saturday. Still, it worked. Kane had a radar for girls. After our second time around the circle, he threw open the window in Declan's room, which was in the front of the house, and said, "You guys out for a stroll?"

I snorted. We were wearing our dress pumps. If that wasn't desperate, the twelve new blisters crying out for mercy from my toes and heels definitely were. But Luisa had that innocent way about her—even when she was up to no good, she still reeked of sunshine. I yawned, glad that he was finally here. Luisa and Kane could say hey, share a few flirts, and then we could haul ass to bed.

He pushed up the window and slid out on the roof, then climbed down the rain gutter and trellis to the front porch. Luisa watched this feat in amazement. "He's gonna kill himself."

"It's not that hard," I told her. "I've climbed up there a million times."

Her eyes shifted to me and narrowed a little. This was clearly not news she'd wanted to hear.

"The best view of the fireworks in Trum is from his rooftop," I added in explanation.

Bounding over to us, Kane said, "What is this? A party I wasn't invited to?"

Luisa giggled. She could not stop giggling when Kane was concerned. I had to tell her boys like you a hell of a lot more when you pretend they don't exist. "Oh, you're definitely invited!" she gushed.

Somehow the decision was made to go to the woods out back, with the ancient broken-down tree house and a fire pit that must've been built by the house's previous occupants. Such a decision was not made with my consent, but by that time, I didn't even exist to register a vote. Kane and Luisa were already in their own impenetrable, perfect Kane-and-Luisa bubble. So I yawned some more and told her I'd leave the back door unlocked.

She didn't come back inside until after three. She refused to say much about what they were doing, but she mentioned that Kane's dad had finally sent Declan to fetch them. "They're both gorgeous, Hail! Why didn't you tell me?" she'd said that morning. "You are more than the luckiest girl in school. I'd kill to live where you do."

Friday, February 15

MORNING

As usual, I wake up with a stomachache. That's what I take to school with me these days, instead of lunch money. That, and a bottle of…water.

Kane meets me at the car as I pile my books into the back seat and set my water bottle in the console. Before I know it, he's unscrewing the top. He takes a sniff. "Just checking," he says.

I yank it from him and tighten the lid. "Who are you, my mother?"

"I'm your passenger. And I don't want you driving if you've been hitting the sauce."

I try to start the Jeep. It stalls a couple times in the cold before roaring to life. Kane doesn't know me anymore. He likes to think he does, but I have changed. And spending a couple minutes every day in the passenger seat of my Jeep won't make him a Hailey expert.

Coming back to Deer Hills three months into the school year is hard enough when you don't have memories of your dead boyfriend haunting you. I'd kept up with schoolwork at the hospital and came back the week of Thanksgiving because Juliet said a short week would make reentry less stressful.

Wrong.

So by the Tuesday before Thanksgiving, I'd started self-medicating, taking sips from my mom's Absolut supply. It worked fine—in fact, too fine. I'd liked how it numbed me so much that I started upping my dose.

And so I got in a little trouble. Okay, more than a little trouble, since it happened twice. The first time, Principal Williams said that because of all I'd endured, he'd let me slide. The second time, he said that because of all I'd endured, he'd let me slide, but there'd better not be a third time, or I'd be welcomed to Suspension City.

There hasn't been a third time. Yet.

Until last year, I hadn't so much as looked at a teacher the wrong way. I was the good girl: Student Council representative, Key Club president, girlfriend to the esteemed Declan Weeks. Now, I'm none of those things.

Not a single one.

Instead I'm a Cheez-It chomping, vodka-guzzling loner.

I think of when I was younger. I wanted a talent so bad it about killed me. Everyone had one, but me? Nothing. When I'd confessed this to Declan, he'd said my *thing* was being me, and being his. He'd told me that if I could juggle knives or sing beautifully or whatever, I wouldn't be his Hailey. At the time, I'd melted.

Now, I'm no one.

I look over at Kane. If they took before and after pictures of us, mine would be a total one-eighty. His, mirror images. It's so mystifying that I forget to upshift to third as we pull onto the main road.

"Whoa, babe," Kane says, nearly putting his hand on mine as I struggle with the clutch. Then he thinks better of it and pulls away. He studies me. "If Williams sees you're drunk—"

"I'm not!" I shout at him, then lean forward and breathe heavily in his face. "Happy?"

"Minty fresh. But, you know, vodka is odorless."

"No, it's not."

We pull into the senior parking lot, where Luisa is waiting by my usual space. Before, she used to wait at the front of the bus line for me. Now, when Kane hops out of the car, she hooks an arm through his and starts to pull him toward the front of the school before I can gather my stuff out of the back seat.

It's Kane who hangs back. He grins at me. "See you, Hail."

Luisa looks back at the Jeep and seems surprised to see me

there. "Hey, Hail." Then she tilts Kane's chin toward her, her eyes begging so he has no choice but to kiss her. He must've done *something* for her last night, judging from the way she can't keep her hands off him. I don't want to think of what.

He probably flashed that smile of his. The kid is lethal that way.

But the two of them together? Super lethal. Pale people can go one of two ways: either veiny, uncooked chicken flesh or perfect, porcelain china doll. Luisa's the latter—skin so white and milky, with pale, barely-there eyelashes and hair. She's not the type to suffer sunburns. Luisa is too prepared for that. Plus, she's brilliant—straight As, ever since elementary school. She's the person you'd hate if she didn't have an innocent, sweet, soft way of talking and look like a freaking angel placed directly on this earth by the hand of God. Our falling-out—or drifting apart, whatever it was—would never be attributed to her. It's all on me, the girl who lost her boyfriend and, subsequently, her mind.

I never knew what people meant when they said a thing was "greater than the sum of one's parts." But that's Luisa and Kane. Enviable on their own, but as a couple, they rule.

I have no choice but to trail behind them like the court jester. I think about how Luisa used to always sleep over at my house when we were younger. Most of the time, we'd talk and giggle about boys, wondering what two specific boys were up to across the street. I never slept over at her house, even though she had a much ritzier home with an in-ground pool. There was something more exciting about being so close to two gorgeous brothers. As we got older, the four of us would light fires in the old fire pit and hang out in the woods behind the cul-de-sac on warm summer nights. I'd almost think Luisa was using me if I hadn't known her well before boys became interesting.

I shiver and blame the chill on this bleak, seemingly endless winter.

When we get to the school, Kane holds the door open for me. As I pass through, I think about the picture Declan's mother gave me. THIS ENDS HERE. I'm about to tell him about it when he whispers, "Take it easy, okay, Hail?" and then he sweeps Luisa back into his arms.

Take it easy. The way he says it is not a casual send-off. It's full of caution and worry. Because it's par for the course for me to take everything hard.

At my locker, I see Javier and Nina. Javier is my locker neighbor, and you'll rarely see Javier without Nina. They're the last third of our sextet. Javier transferred to Deer Hills from Spain during the middle of his sophomore year and barely spoke English, so Kane was elected to help him around school. Since Javier and Declan were the only new kids at Deer Hills, they quickly became friends. Nina was always Luisa's friend because they live in the same neighborhood and went to dance class together.

Because the six of us always hung out together, eventually Nina and Javier became a couple. Kane may complain about Luisa in secret to me, but Javier and Nina have the opposite dynamic. They *constantly* look like they can't stand each other. Their fights are explosive, the result of being two people who probably never would've gotten together if it weren't for us pushing them that way.

They're at each other's throats again. Nina's dark cheeks are flushed, and she's scowling. She grabs my arm as I approach and says, "Oh good, Hailey. Tell him."

I run the dial on my lock, cursing when I can't remember the numbers. Details I know by heart leak away, somehow. Finally I pull open my locker and look over at Nina, who is looking at me expectantly.

Nina has a habit of thinking people can read her mind. "Tell him what?"

She sighs. "That you can't go naked under your cap and gown."

I raise my eyebrow at Javier, happy to have something *else* to talk about.

He grins at me. He usually says shit like this to get Nina riled up, and even after more than a year together, she still hasn't wised up to the ploy. Nina is more serious than a heart attack. Javier says, his accent thick, "Oh come on, Nee. It's going to be hot under there."

I don't have to look at him. From his tone of voice, I can tell he's kidding. I get my books for first period and say, "He can if he wants to. But I think the fabric is kind of sheer. We might see your junk."

She screws up her face. "God forbid. No one wants to see your junk."

Javier nods. "But my junk is so impressive, no?"

She punches him. "You wish."

He grabs his arm and winces. Overpowered by a girl who's half his size and probably weighs ninety pounds soaking wet? Javier is the biggest wimp ever. "Come on, Nee. I was kidding. *Mi madre* bought me a three-piece suit with a top hat, *un reloj de bolsillo, y un monóculo.* Happy?"

"I have no idea what that is, but it sounds better." She smiles and smooths her shiny, black pixie hair as I slam my locker door. When I look back up, she's peering at me in a very familiar way. Javier is too. Nina's father is a police officer and was first on the scene when Mrs. Weeks called 911 about Declan. It's highly likely Mr. Paradis shielded his daughter from the most gruesome details, but I can't help thinking that she knows more about what happened that day than all of us, simply because of her connections.

I wince, waiting for it. The two of them exchange glances, daring each other to broach the subject first, so I say, "Nice talking to you," and turn to make my escape.

Nina hooks my arm in hers and walks with me toward first

period. "Really. We just want to know how you are. You know. Because of everything."

Because of everything. It occurs to me that she can't zero in on one thing because everything in my life is shit. "*Everything*"—I emphasize the word—"is fine."

"You were okay yesterday?"

I take a sip of my water. "Sure. Easy-peasy."

She touches my water bottle. "So, what's that?" she singsongs.

I sigh. "Water. Really." I ignore the fact that she's leaning in, probably to smell my breath. "Geez. Can't I make a mistake once without everyone getting on me for it?"

Javier falls in line behind us. "It was twice."

"Thank you for keeping score, Jav," I grumble. They're not the only ones taking an interest in my water bottle. Mr. Vanderbilt, my chem teacher, watches from the door of his classroom. It's hazy, but I think I fell shitfaced off one of the stools in his lab before Christmas and he had to carry me to the nurse's while I drifted in and out of consciousness.

"Fine. You know what?" I stalk past a trash can and drop the bottle in it. "I'd rather dehydrate like a sad raisin than hear it from you guys."

I try to be light and fun about it, grinning, but there's this underlying tension to my voice. The more I push for normalcy, the less I succeed. "You look tired," Nina observes.

"I never wear makeup first thing. Gym," I tell her. Or at least that's what I tell everyone. It doesn't make sense to dress up first thing when I'm going to have to change into sweats and run the track. But really, I haven't put much into my appearance for a long time. The meds have wreaked havoc on my body, making my skin break out, adding pounds... I know I look different, but I'm here, at least. I make a mental note to put on some lip gloss when I change into my school outfit. "So what's the deal? You guys have a good Valentine's Day?"

Nina and Javier exchange worried glances. I don't know who issued the command that the V-holiday couldn't be mentioned in my presence. I brought it up, after all. Finally, Nina says, "Um, fine." Then she quickly adds, "Did you do that problem set for trig?"

I might never have been the class clown, but people used to joke with me. They used to have fun around me. Now, I can't get through a conversation without awkward silences and half-uttered sentences. "Yeah," I answer. "It sucked."

Trig is usually easy for me. But last night, it wasn't. Every two seconds, my eyes would wander to that Yuengling box filled with Declan's stuff. It had seen his last moments. Those moments before he went down into the basement and pulled Mr. Weeks's handgun out of its case. Before he'd gone out to the shed, broken open the lock, and...

Before, we used to go to the movies at least once a month. To the diner. To the mall. As six, it worked out nicely. We'd all pile into Javier's SUV. Now, we're an odd five. We haven't been anywhere as a group in more than a year. The last time, we'd gone to see some forgettable comedy that wasn't worth the price of admission. It was such a low-note ending. Like Declan's last tweet, a day before: *Wawa packed with people getting bread and milk. Couldn't get gas.*

Not exactly profound.

All of it was so dull, so everyday. In fact, nothing he had done said, *This is my last.*

When I break out of my trance, Nina and Javier are staring at me. It's obvious Nina asked me another question while I was spaced out. "Huh?" I ask.

Nina massages my shoulder. "I was asking if you heard what happened with Luisa and Kane. I heard they had a real big blowout yesterday."

The six of used to hang out before first period in front of my locker and Javier's, since they were central to our classes. But that changed last year. Luisa and Kane usually go off on their own to who-knows-where, and I barely see them throughout the day. "That's old news," I mumble. "I saw them this morning. They're fine."

"Oh. Really? Well, that's boring. She's a total bitch anyway, ignoring us like she does."

Not ignoring us. Ignoring *me* is more like it.

I tell Nina I'll see her in trig and head off toward the locker rooms, my mind swirling more than ever. Juliet said that I'd think about him less and less as time went on, but she failed to tell me that every anniversary—of our first kiss, our first date—would stir up the memories afresh.

IT ENDS HERE.

Yes, if by "it" you mean everything normal about my life. It all ended that day. These days, I'm the odd girl out. The leftover. Maybe I'll never be anything else.

Gym is my least favorite class because I don't have a single ally there anymore. I used to be...not *popular,* but someone who held her own. Popular seniors wouldn't be buddy-buddy with me, but they'd talk to me here and there. Now, they turn the other way when I come near.

They don't know what to say, so they avoid, avoid, avoid.

It's probably good, since even the stupidest, silliest comments have a way of reducing me to tears. Declan was the brain, the thinker. He wanted to go into engineering and architecture— urban planning, he thought. He was constantly working with his hands, getting them all cut up building models. At any time, he'd have half a dozen bandages on his hands. So a couple months ago, when I got a paper cut in art, I started to sob uncontrollably when the teacher offered me a Band-Aid.

No wonder they all expect me to have a mental breakdown. It wouldn't be the first time.

I trudge into the locker room, and the smell of body odor and baby powder assaults my nose. Everyone in my row stops and looks at me as I sit on the bench and bend over, taking my combination lock in my hand. I spin the lock face, trying to clear my mind so that I can focus on the numbers.

IT ENDS HERE.

Not the pain. Juliet was wrong. The pain grows. It grows and stretches until it's bigger than me. It's spiraling out, and sometimes I can feel it not only in my chest, but radiating out of my arms and legs, suffocating me and everything around me.

That feeling comes, silent and dark as fog. Before I can channel one of Juliet's coping techniques, it settles over my mind, extinguishing all but one thought there.

Bleed.

Cut yourself, and bleed.

Bleed. Declan bled out too. I'd joked that he was the Gentle Californian Soul, but nothing about his death was gentle. I didn't see much, but in my mind, he's crouched in the corner of the shed, his head reduced to nothing but globs of flesh and shards of bone sprayed out onto the particleboard wall like a child's excited finger painting. He reduced the shed to something so grotesque and irreparable that the only solution was for his father to burn the damn thing to the ground.

Declan never did anything half-assed. Go big or go home.

Me, however? I was always the wishy-washy one. The *I don't know, what do you want to do?* type. I never had an opinion. The scars on my wrists have become chicken scratches, half-hearted cries for help.

Mrs. Wilbur calls everyone out to the gym. The others file out, their voices fading away, leaving me with the sounds of the whirring of the fans above me.

I finally pull open the lock and look at my hands. They're white and trembling. I spy it on the ground. A flash of silver. Someone left a nail file. I pick it up. I feel like it's here for a reason.

There is a reason for everything.

And that reason is still haunting me every damn day: Declan.

Using the faint, raised scar on my wrist as a guide, I watch the blood bubble up as I begin to slice.

514 Days Before

Once upon a time, my parents liked each other.

But I sure as hell couldn't remember it. That's why I spent most of my time outside, away from the demilitarized zone.

I got another splinter climbing up the pirate-ship playhouse in the giant swing set behind my house. The thing hadn't been varnished in years. It was the part of summer that dips its foot into September, and when I wasn't in school, I was milking the last of the warm weather, wearing short-shorts and going barefoot. Mosquito bites and scrapes riddled my body. I didn't mind. I liked sitting up in the playhouse, feeling the breeze and watching the ducks play in the retention pond below me.

Tucked in the corner of the yard, at least I couldn't hear the arguing. This time, my dad was getting it because he'd bought the wrong kind of taco meat at the store. Last time, my mom got it because she'd thrown away my dad's favorite shirt, which was full of holes. It always started with something small, then escalated to all-out war.

I'd brought my sketchbook with me, even though I sucked at drawing. I wasn't good at anything, sadly—not even dance, though I'd done that after gymnastics, which I started when I was three. I'd also tried softball, clarinet, soccer… None of it stuck. Kane said the same thing my parents said: that I got bored with things too easily. But after working so hard with dance only to constantly lag behind the other girls, I wanted to be a natural at something.

I wanted a talent.

I leaned back against the ship's wheel, stretched out my black-and-blue legs, and swept the pencil over the paper, liking the scratchy sound it made.

"Hey," a voice said.

Startled, I dropped my pencil. His black hair was wet, as if he'd just gone swimming, and he was barefoot, wearing nothing but shorts. He'd already started climbing up the rock-wall rope toward me. I pulled my knees up to my chest as he reached me. He slid in easily and draped his long legs over the side.

"You writing?"

I clutched the notebook to my chest and wiped a stray hair from my braid over my head. I'd slept in that braid, which meant my hair had to be a horror. "Just drawing."

I hadn't seen Declan since he'd moved in earlier that summer. He'd started his junior year of high school in a completely different world from the freshmen and sophomore building. His arrival at Kane's house had come with a tarp-covered *something*—a truck, I'd guessed by the shape, which took up much of the one-car driveway. Sometimes I'd see a set of big feet poking out from under the chassis.

His arrival also meant that Kane was at my house a whole lot more. Well, at first. In the beginning, Kane did nothing but complain. *He eats all the food in the house. His mom makes me do shit, like make my bed. They act like they own the place.* But as Declan climbed up, I realized I hadn't seen Kane much in the past week. When I had seen him, he'd been so tired from baseball practice that he hadn't complained once.

"Can I see?" he asked.

My heart thrummed. I buried the sketchbook in my lap. "No."

He looked out over the retention pond, which was dry, baring its pasty bottom. A couple of geese plodded along the bank, oblivious to us. He watched them, and I used the time to study his profile. Luisa was definitely right. He had a strong jaw, a little bit of uneven, dark stubble too. There was a small scar over his eye, like a little red star. His arms were muscular, his chest dark and lean, with awkward angles that showed the promise of more. He was almost seventeen. Older. The only older boy I knew.

And Kane's stepbrother. That meant Declan was probably off-limits.

Which, of course, made me fall for him instantly. I can't explain it. One second I was totally aloof, annoyed that he'd invade my personal space. The next, I felt a giddiness I hadn't known. He'd played guitar for me, and I'd thought he was okay. He was exciting—like that new outfit you can't wait to wear to school. Geeky, but not repellent, as were so many boys at school. Suddenly, I felt a flicker of desperation, like *please stay*.

His eyes scanned my scabby legs. I hugged them to my chest, covering them with my arms, then wondered if my underwear was visible, peeking out of my Daisy Dukes. I quickly threw my legs over the side of the platform. "Um…how do you like Pennsy?"

His gaze hovered on my bruised knees. "'Sokay. Some things pale in comparison."

I blushed, thinking he was talking about me, to be specific. I'd been to California once, for a family trip when I was twelve. All the girls there were impossibly skinny and smooth-skinned and plastic. And here I was, a giant scab with unruly hair.

"For example," he went on, "no In-N-Out Burger. What's with that? I have to eat at Wendy's. Not the same."

I relaxed. "Oh. You're lucky you survived. That stuff can kill a gentle Californian soul like yours."

He grinned, then leaned back on his elbows, staring up at the shredded green tarp overhead. "It's nice here, though." Then he sat up and jumped to the ground. He eased down into one of the swings and nodded his chin at me. "You swing?"

I put down my notebook, climbed down, and sat on the swing next to him. It was the most weight that old swing set had seen in a long time, so it groaned as we started to pump our legs and drive toward the sky.

"How long have you known him?" he asked.

"Kane?" *Well, duh, Hailey, who else?* "Oh. Forever, I guess. I mean, we've lived across the street from each other all our lives. And he always sits behind me in school, because I'm Ward, and he's Weeks. He used to pull my pigtails and stuff. But we didn't really become friends until third grade. All the kids were calling me Hurly and making throw-up sounds around me. He beat them up."

"Defended your honor, huh?"

"Not really. I think he wanted to be the only one to pick on me."

Declan laughed. "That sounds like him. Funny kid."

I snorted. "Kid? He's a year younger than you."

"Nine months." He grinned. "The devil is in the details with us gentle Californian souls. Plus, I've always wanted a kid brother."

"You guys must be getting along better. He hasn't come over to my house with his mopey face in at least twenty-four hours."

He smiled. "What, that disappoints you?"

Truthfully, I *had* been disappointed. A little. I wouldn't call myself possessive, but Kane was like a favorite pair of jeans that I'd outgrown but still couldn't bear to give away. "No," I said. "I mean—"

"Are you guys together?"

"Together as in…together?" *Um, yeah, really bright, Hailey.* "No. No. No. No. Kane is…Kane. He changes girls more often than he changes his socks."

"Oh yeah? So my kid brother is a player, huh? Interesting." He dragged his feet on the ground to stop swinging, so I did too. When he jumped off the swing, he turned to me. "I get the feeling you can teach me a lot, young Hailey."

I nearly swooned at the way he said my name. He spoke slowly, always, but he said it in a singsong, breathy way that I felt all the way down to my toes. "What do you want to know?"

He shrugged. Then he reached through the wooden slats of the pirate ship and pulled out my notebook. I cringed as he looked at the picture I'd drawn. I'd only managed a few horizontal lines, with small peaks meant to be the ducks swimming across the pond.

He said, "Impressive." Then he climbed up into the ship and put a pencil to the paper. "You mind?"

"Whatever. I was only playing around."

He started to sweep the pencil across the page. His dark hair fell in his eyes, and he blew it out of the way, pushed those dark frames up the bridge of his nose. The concentration on his face was delicious; I couldn't look away. I couldn't formulate words.

"So," he said, glancing at me, making me blush because he must've known how intently I was studying him. "Hailey Ward. What else do you like to do?"

I'd started playing with a button on my tank top. When I recognized what I was doing, calling attention to that area of my anatomy, I stopped abruptly and fastened my hands against my sides. Flat as a pancake. That's what Kane called me. Quickly, I crossed my arms over my chest. Better. "Gymnastics?" I don't know why it came out as a question.

"Really? Can you do a cartwheel?"

I nodded.

"Do one."

"What, now?"

He nodded.

I turned out into the grassy part of the lawn and did one. Then, because I felt like showing off, I did a front handspring. A terrible, wobbly one, because halfway into it, the bottom of my tank top sagged, exposing my stomach and threatening to reveal all I *didn't* have. When I landed, I tucked the hem of my shirt into my shorts. "Happy?"

He nodded. Then he passed the picture over to me. He hadn't

been adding to my sketch. Instead, there were a few sparse, curved lines, but together they made a picture of a pretty girl in profile…a girl with a braid. Me. It made my duck picture look like a kindergartner's project. I sucked my bottom lip into my mouth. Of course *he* had a thing. He had more than one, considering how well he played the guitar. "You're talented."

"Eh," he said, breathing on his fingernails and pretending to buff them on his chest. "You are too. That was the best…flippy thing I've ever seen."

"Handspring. Thanks," I said. "But I'm terrible, compared to the kids in my class. I stopped going. Took up dance."

"Dance, huh? Like ballet?"

I nodded, then admitted, "But I'm not really great at that, either."

Then we kind of stood there, staring at each other. My heart was going a million miles an hour. When the silence was broken, it was by both of us. We exploded with words at the exact same time. I asked, "So where is he?" and he said, "So maybe…"

Then we tittered in unison, and my face went hot. "Um, what?"

He shook his head, swallowing back whatever he was going to say. I silently cursed as he switched directions and said, "Camp. Some sports thing? Soccer? Baseball?"

"Oh. Baseball." That was Kane's *thing*.

He shrugged. "I can't remember. Or maybe he's at his tutor? His dad said if he didn't get his grades up, he wouldn't be playing."

That was true. Kane was smart, but not book-smart. He had a solid C average. The same threat loomed over him every year: get the grades up, or no sports. "You're not a sports person?"

"Nah." He thrust his hand into mine. "I have gentle Californian hands. See?"

His hands were twice the size of mine; I could feel calluses in the palms, and he had an old Band-Aid, black and frayed on the edges, wrapped tight around one knuckle. But it wasn't unpleasant. Oh lordy, it was quite the opposite of unpleasant. I'd never held a boy's hand before, but I wanted to start, right then, and make sure all the rest of my days were filled with more hand-holding. Instead, I casually lifted one of his big hands and inspected it as if it were a cantaloupe I was thinking of buying at the grocer's, trying to fight back the goose bumps and shivers of excitement springing out all over my body. "Ah, yes. Smooth as a baby's butt."

He narrowed his eyes. "Are you comparing me to a baby's butt?"

"No. Just your hands."

"Awesome."

He smiled as I released his hand. Another long silence passed between us, and this time it was enough for the awkwardness to completely settle in. "I've got to go," I told him, hoping my parents had called a truce. "We... I have somewhere to be." I was embarrassed to say where.

"Oh," he said, disappointed. "What time is it?"

"Like four, maybe?"

"Oh. I've got somewhere to be too." He jogged away, then bent down and slid his body between the logs of the fence that surrounded our property. He didn't look back.

"See you later, alligator," he sang when he was on the other side. I breathed hard as I walked back to my house, his musical voice ringing in my ears.

It was still ringing in my ears as my parents and I slid into the pew at church that night. My parents were both tense. I stood between them, going through the motions: lazily crossing myself, bowing my head, mumbling prayers, and fudging verses I didn't know—pretending to be a good little Catholic. My parents went to church because that's what they'd been raised to do. Sometimes we missed mass, sometimes we showed up in less than our Sunday best, sometimes we didn't have anything to put in the collection basket, and we hadn't been to confession in years, despite all the sins we'd piled up. And we always skipped out after communion. It was about convenience: if there was something better to do, we did that instead.

Truthfully, I only went to church when my parents insisted. I wasn't religious. I knew my parents were staying together, as miserable as they were, partly because they were raised to believe that divorce was a sin, but mostly because they were comfortable in their misery. I didn't think there was an afterlife waiting for me. I didn't think God existed. I hated the fact that all these good Catholics would sit there and pray and sing and listen to Father Brady talk about the Golden Rule, then cut each other off trying to be the first ones to leave the parking lot.

What I thought was, *You don't need God to be good, and some people who follow God blindly are the worst.*

But that night something happened. When the music started and the procession came down the center aisle, who was first in line, holding the cross? Declan Weeks. I blinked, as if my vision would clear and reveal him to be a mirage. But there he was, in a white robe, climbing the stairs to the altar. He bowed, then turned, and his eyes swept over me for the briefest of moments.

I looked around and saw his mother sitting in the first pew, the suck-up-to-God pew. My parents and I were dressed in shorts, and I still hadn't taken my hair out of that nightmare braid. The new Mrs. Weeks was pretty and blond and wearing a pastel dress that reeked of Easter Sunday.

I thought Declan might give me a goofy grin, a little wave— but he didn't. He did his job the proper way. He looked serene and dignified. He bowed fully and respectfully, sang all the verses loudly and without fudging the words. I know this, because though he never looked at me, my eyes rarely left him. By the time the homily rolled around and he took his seat behind the priest, I felt like an imposter in the church where I'd been baptized.

But I didn't want to seem uncomfortable with Declan there, so when my parents made to leave after communion, I made a beeline back to our pew, saying with a whisper, "Let's stay."

My parents usually did everything possible to avoid shaking hands with the priest at the end of mass. As we were skirting around him, we ran straight into Declan and his mother.

My mom was her usual overly polite self. "Oh, it's wonderful to see you two," she said. "We were just saying how we should have you all over to dinner to get better acquainted."

We weren't. But she looked at my dad and me for affirmation, and we bobbed our heads eagerly in agreement.

Declan had shed his robe and was wearing nice khakis and a button-down shirt. I flattened my hair and pulled at my frayed Daisy Dukes as we walked with them to the parking lot.

I said, "I didn't know you were Catholic."

He said, "Yep. I've had eight years of Catholic school. This is my first year going to public."

"Oh. That's…nice." *Intimidating* was what I was thinking. I don't think Kane and his dad had ever set foot in a church. Well, I guess his dad and mom got married in one, but they'd divorced ages ago. "Your parents are divorced?"

"Nah. My dad died three years ago." Before I could feel guilty about bringing up the subject, he added, "But it's okay. Our faith got us through it."

I was completely dumbstruck. People who talked about faith usually freaked me out. Like, how could anyone believe so strongly in something you couldn't touch or see? But him? I wanted to ask Declan more. Someone like him could maybe get me to believe too.

Instead, I chewed on my lip, afraid I might say something to offend his godly ways.

"Anyway," Declan said as we reached my parents' Volvo, as if he'd been carrying on an entire conversation with me in his head. That was the thing about Declan—he didn't do awkward silences. When he was silent, there was a good reason for it.

We stopped and turned; our parents were still standing and talking at the entrance of the church. I shivered because it was getting chilly as it was getting darker. "Catch you at home?"

"Yeah."

His eyes lingered on me. I held my breath, wondering if he could see through me, straight to my sins.

Friday, February 15

"You have such pretty eyes," Nurse Ryan tells me as she wraps my wrist.

I'm glad she's so mesmerized by my baby blues. I'm glad it's her and not Nurse Fielding, who retired last year after twenty years with Deer Hills. Nurse Fielding was a ballbuster. She wouldn't bandage a hangnail without a game of twenty questions. Even though Nurse Ryan winds the bandage too tightly, she doesn't notice the similar cuts up higher near my elbow.

Hooray for ignorance. Hooray for long sleeves. Freaking hallelujah.

Hooray too for a gym teacher who only cares about collecting a paycheck. Wilbur caught Declan and me making out under the bleachers in the gym once and didn't say anything. But today, as the blood pooled atop my wrist and then coursed down through my fingers onto the lacquered gym floor, Wilbur handed me the hall pass and an inadequate wad of tissues and ushered me out the door. I'd had the *cut it on the locker door* excuse on the tip of my tongue, but she didn't even wait to hear it.

"I cut it on the locker door," I blurt out to Nurse Ryan. Apparently, the excuse had been fighting to get out all this time.

The young nurse nods as she peels a piece of surgical tape and secures it. "All fixed." She's blond and cheerful, and I know she means well. "We should have a janitor take a look at it."

I stare at her.

"At the locker, of course. Not your arm." She giggles as if she's twelve.

I pull my sleeve over the bandage so it's hardly noticeable. I threw away the file. Good as new. "Sure."

"What the hell? Are you okay?"

I know it's Kane before he speaks, before I turn around. I cringe. I'd expected this. News travels fast in this school.

He kneels in front of the cot and looks at my bandage. "Shit, Hail. Shit."

The nurse crosses her arms. "She's fine. What class are you coming from? You need to—"

"You don't know her. I need to make sure my friend is all right," he snaps, giving her a hard stare that almost makes me feel bad for her. She clearly has no idea who she's up against. She opens her mouth to respond, but then stops. Kane has that way about him. People listen to him.

He obviously feels bad for snapping, though, because a second later, he says gently, "I'll walk her to her class, if that's all right with you?"

The nurse nods and hands me a pass. "I'll have a janitor look into that locker. What number?"

I glance at Kane, then back at her. "Oh. Um. Five thirteen."

We walk into the hallway, and he turns to me, putting both hands on my shoulders. "What? You told her you cut your wrist on a locker? And she bought that?"

"I *did*," I insist.

"Right, and in the exact same place where…" He runs his hands through his hair. He's not buying it. "You need to stop this, Hail. You want to go back to Shady Harbor?"

I can't meet his eyes.

"Hail. You have to move on. You can't do this. You know Declan would want that." He picks up my wrist and lets it fall, disgusted. "I mean, you were good at gymnastics. Dance. If you just took a few—"

"Stop," I mutter. Dancing is the last thing on my mind. My muscle tone is so nonexistent that I'd probably fall over if I tried to do a cartwheel or get back on pointe again. "Give it up. You're not Mr. Fix-It."

No, that was Declan. Suddenly I flash back to the first time Declan came to my dance class. He'd shown up with Kane, who'd come to pick me up. It was the night my grandmother died, and Kane hadn't understood how upset I was. Declan had. Declan, who barely knew me, understood me a million times better, even then.

"Well, it's clear someone has to help you, and it's not going to be Declan."

I scowl at Kane who's pulled me back to the present. "You have no idea. You didn't know him like I did."

He laughs. "Yeah, we were only stepbrothers for two years. We shared a roof, and that's all."

I pull away and start down the hallway. I've always been the weak one, the one who cared too much. Then I whirl around and nearly smack into his broad chest. I hadn't realized he was so close. I take a step back. "Why did he do it?" I murmur.

He strains forward, as if trying to hear me better. "Come on, Hail, don't—"

"Why?" My voice is louder and stronger.

He exhales again and shrugs, digging his hands into the pockets of his jeans. "I don't know. Stress? He was stressed trying to get into college."

That's what they said anyway. Sure, Declan cared about grades. He was brilliant, so his grades were there. He applied to ten schools, UPenn being his dream, and a number of safe ones too. After he died, the big, fat envelopes came rolling in. He'd gotten accepted to every one of them—even UPenn. "He had no reason to stress," I say.

"What?"

"He had no reason to stress," I repeat, louder. "All the applications were in. The hard part was over. I mean, all he was doing was waiting."

"Okay, but it's over. It happened. We can't bring him back."

"But I can try to *understand* it, Kane. And I don't. That's why I can't move on. So bear with me. I mean, what did he say to you the last time you saw him?"

"You're a masochist, you know that? I saw him the night before he died. I don't know when you saw him last, but what does it matter?"

We have been over it. In the weeks following his death, we all had discussed the whys and hows until the horror of it numbed us. But the details had blurred with time.

He tugs my sleeve. "You need to get back to class before someone calls out the guards on you."

"What about you?" I ask, already knowing the answer. Kane is above the rules. People gladly bend restrictions and make exceptions where he's concerned. His crazy best friend? They keep extra eyes on me.

We walk down the hallway in relative silence until I can't take it any longer. I hug my notebook to my chest and say, "I'm sorry.

I know I should forget it. But yesterday was so weird…and when your mom wanted to give me his things…I saw that picture, and I just…snapped. I'm sorry."

He stares at me, his expression softening. "What picture?"

I reach into my purse and pull it out, hand it to him.

He looks at it for a second, then shoves it back into the envelope. "Where did you get this?"

"Your stepmom. She said she found it in his room."

"And you have no idea what this is?"

"Why? Should I?" I reach over to take it back from him. He yanks it away. Then he holds it over his head and starts laughing at me as I jump to try to grab it from him. "Give it back," I tell him.

"Why?" he asks. "Why does it matter?"

He crumples it in his fist, then thinks better of it and starts to rip it up. It doesn't tear well, but he shoves it in a trash can, deep, and throws some paper on top.

"Kane! What are you doing that for?"

He shrugs. "Because you don't need it. You should take that entire box she gave you and burn it. You need to move forward."

I study the trash can. "But it could be important. I mean… why else would he keep it? It looks like… I don't know." I walk over to the trash can and peer inside, but the photo is lost in a sea of paper. "What if someone was threatening him?"

Kane lets out a snort, as if he doesn't believe me. Then he

realizes I'm serious. "Hail, come on. Do you realize what you're saying?"

It's true. Declan was too good for that. "Well, maybe—"

"Hail! Enough. It won't change that Declan is gone. You can't dwell on the details. You think rehashing everything about that night will help you? How? What'll help you is moving on. You shouldn't have bailed on all your activities this year. You clearly need something else to occupy your mind."

I stare at him. "All right," I say. "I'm sorry."

We reach the door to the gymnasium. He puts up a hand as if he's going to touch my arm, but pulls back and rakes his hair behind his ear. He stoops to look into my eyes. "You going to be okay?"

I force a smile. "Yeah," I say.

"No freaking out on me now, okay? If you feel bad, text me or something. Okay?"

Text me or something. My hero.

I pull open the door to the gymnasium. It feels as if everyone turns and looks at me. Balls stop bouncing, conversations end, bodies freeze. The only sound is the squeak of my sneakers on the polished floor. Wilbur tells me to sit on the bleachers for the rest of the period and shouts at everyone, "Move it!"

Class resumes, life resumes, everything goes on but Hailey Ward. And when I look back for Kane, he's already gone.

478 Days Before

When school started up, it meant that dance started up again.

My mom had it in her head that I could be a professional gymnast or dancer. Why else had she brought me to Grace Gymnastics & Dance Center four days a week since the time I was three?

I'd started with gymnastics, but quickly moved to dance when I fell behind my teammates. I didn't possess Luisa and Nina's flexibility. My mother would watch me from the observation room, and sometimes she'd look disappointed. *Practice makes perfect*, she told me time and again. But all of that practice only made it clear that there were some moves I'd never be able to do. Like a split. My legs simply didn't go that way. Some things were a matter of natural talent.

The further I went with dance, the more inadequate I felt.

"You did just fine," Luisa said, massaging my shoulder as I slinked toward our cubbies and started to untie my pointe shoes.

Usually I agreed with her, because there was no point in arguing. But I was fed up with her lying to me to make me feel better. I was bitter too. We'd gotten our PSAT scores back, and while Luisa had scored in the 1400s and Nina had gotten a 1200, I hadn't broken 1000. Kane was the only one who hadn't beat me, but he treated those tests like a joke. I'd taken mine as though my life depended on it, ensuring I'd had the required number two pencils and gotten a good night's sleep. So I felt like a massive goober.

"I didn't do fine," I snapped at her, feeling bad the second the words were out. I sighed and threw on my hoodie. "I sucked. You can be honest."

"It doesn't matter," Nina said. "Miss Amber always gives good parts to everyone for *The Nutcracker*."

Yes, she always gave out good parts, but I hadn't yet had a solo. Nina and Luisa had both proven their worthiness to Miss Amber. Nina had had a solo since she was ten. She'd been Clara two years ago, and Luisa was Clara last year. So I thought this was my year. But here I was, almost sixteen, and after the mess I made of my tryout, I was likely to be skipped over once again. My humiliation would undoubtedly be accompanied by more maternal disappointment and a serious discussion over whether the three hundred dollars a month was well spent if I insisted on playing around instead of taking dance seriously.

We packed our things and stepped outside, where the moms usually waited for the older kids in the parking lot.

But when we got out there, Kane and Declan were sitting on the benches.

"Ladies," Kane said, tipping an imaginary hat like a dork.

Luisa got all giggly. She tucked her blond hair behind her ear, and her pale skin bloomed red. "Oh, hi! What're you guys here for?"

Kane always knew how to get her. "You," he said, his voice cool, eyes never leaving her face. "Okay?"

She nodded and almost visibly swooned into him. Then she looked back at her mom's Range Rover. Her eyes stormed over. "I should go."

Kane knew this. He was such a mind fuck. "Oh. Too bad." He looked at me and winked. "Guess we'll just walk this girl home."

Declan stood and smacked Kane in the back of the head, but the whole time he was looking at me. "Your mom couldn't pick you up. So Kane said he'd walk you back since it's getting dark."

I narrowed my eyes. "Then why are you here?"

He punched Kane in the arm. "I'm walking *him.*"

"Oh." The studio was only a mile or so from our development, through the woods. But not picking me up was weird, even for my mom. She'd seemed fine when she dropped me off, but I never could tell with her. "Where's my mom? Is everything okay?"

Declan nodded.

Luisa got this desperate look in her eye, and I knew she was thinking how lucky I was. "Maybe I can sleep over your house tonight?" she asked me, but I shook my head. Kane was too busy checking out Luisa's butt in the ballet leotard, but I could tell by the way Declan was looking at me that he was worried about something.

"Sorry, Lou. My parents have a thing," I said vaguely.

She stuck out her lower lip in a pout. "All right," she said, motioning to Nina. "See you guys."

As they left, Kane's eyes lingered on their backsides. I punched him. "So, what?" I asked them when the girls had left and we'd started on the path through the woods. "My mom has been driving me and picking me up for ten years. She's never missed."

"Your grandmother," Kane said. "She died."

I stopped walking. I hadn't expected that. She hadn't even been sick. "Oh my God."

"I'm sorry," Declan said. "You guys were close?"

I shook my head. She lived in Vermont, but my mother always talked to her, sometimes for hours, on the phone. My mother never talked to my dad, only to her mom. And my grandmother would send me cards with money in them. The last time I'd seen her was during a weekend skiing trip when I was fourteen. She was nice to me, made the best macaroni and cheese and short-bread cookies. When we left, she'd given me a little sack of them to take home with me. But I'd left them in the sun and the icing melted so badly that I couldn't eat them. I threw them away.

I always assumed I'd get to see her again. But as we walked home, I realized I'd thrown away the last thing my grandmother would ever give me.

Tears came to my eyes, but I did my best to blink them back. Kane was going on and on about Luisa's ass and how fine it'd looked in her leotard. I tried to listen, to be present, but he was so damn annoying. So oblivious! How could he tell me my grandmother died in one breath and be a complete horndog in the next?

"Well, thanks," I murmured when we got to Fox Court.

"I got some math shit to do. See you," Kane said, starting to jog off to his house. But Declan lingered. When Kane realized he wasn't following, he shouted, "Come on, Dec. It's your turn to take out the garbage. You're not putting it on my ass again."

"I'll catch up," he said as Kane headed toward the house. He turned to me. "Are you okay?"

"I've been better." I sighed. "You got your SATs back, didn't you? What did you get?"

"Fifteen-sixty," he said, smiling, clearly pleased with himself.

Ugh. I shouldn't have asked. This day probably couldn't suck more.

His smile dissolved. "What? Why? Oh, hey. Yeah, Kane said he got his results. Didn't do so well?"

I shook my head. Suddenly, someone shouted, "Eight-fifty!" behind us. Kane was doing a triumphant Rocky jog on the front porch. He was such a loser.

We both shook our heads at him, while Declan said, "Well, the PSAT is hard. You're getting used to the format. I didn't do too well on that either."

Something told me Declan "not doing too well" couldn't have been less than a 1400. "Well, Kane sure seems happy with his score. I didn't do much better than him, honestly. And I *tried*."

"That little brother of mine can be a real twit sometimes." Declan smiled. "But there's something else bothering you. What are you thinking about? Your grandmother?"

I shrugged. It was scary how perceptive he could be. Like he knew me, even though he didn't really know me. "I was just thinking that you never know when you'll see someone for the last time. If I'd known that family ski trip was going to be the last time I saw my grandmother, I would've done things differently."

"Like?"

"I don't know. Eaten her cookies. Things like that."

As ridiculous as I sounded, he nodded with understanding. I occurred to me he must've been thinking about his dad.

"Do you ever regret not doing things with your father?" I asked him quietly. "I mean, not having him to talk to?"

He nodded. "Yeah. Whenever I do, I pray."

"Oh." Of course. I hadn't ever prayed like that before. Most of the time, my prayers were like wishes. I turned back to go into the house, but I had to admit, I was curious how he could have lost the most important person in his life and still remain so together. Here I was, about to fall to pieces about a lady who gave me cookies. Gnawing on my lip, I asked, "Can you show me how?"

He raised an eyebrow. "What? Praying?"

I nodded, blushing. "I've never really…you know."

He grabbed my hand and led me to my old swing set, and he knelt behind it, secluded from the rest of the world, facing the retention pond. I followed and dropped to my knees in my pink tights, feeling stupid at first.

He held my hand the whole time. He said, "God, I'd like to introduce you to Hailey." He looked over at me and winked. "He's pleased to know you. But He made you, so He knows you pretty well already."

I blinked, shocked at how relaxed Declan was.

"Hailey's grandmother passed into your care, and she's

77

concerned. She wants to make sure her grandmother knows how much she loves her."

He bent low to the ground and closed his eyes, then stayed there, very still, for a long time. When he sat up, he rolled over onto the grass and smiled at me. "Hailey," he said. "Do you feel it?"

I closed my eyes, and suddenly, I did feel something. Peace. His rough, Band-Aid-covered hand in mine, warm and perfect. It wasn't only the praying. It was him. Declan. He had this way about him. It was like settling into your warm, comfortable bed after a long, tiring day. He made everything seem right.

"I think she's okay about the cookies," I whispered.

He smiled and stroked the rough pad of one of his fingers over my knuckles. "I think so too."

Saturday, February 16

A thin drizzle falls as I navigate down the driveway, past clumps of sad, dingy snow.

I wish winter would make up its mind. Either snow, or don't. None of this depressing rain.

I slide my sneakered foot along the asphalt, testing it. At least it's not icy. I stretch my hams off the curb, touch my toes, and rub the goose bumps from my legs. I pop in my earbuds as Fall Out Boy pumps through my iPhone, then affix my headband over my ears.

A snowball hits me in the knee.

Globs of ice slide down my shin and collect in the rim of my sport sock. *Who the hell—*

Kane. Of course. He's always been half vampire. He saunters up to me, grinning. He's wearing a loose button-down shirt and jeans, wrinkled, no coat. His pale face amplifies the bleariness of his eyes, but he's Kane. And Kane always looks good.

I scowl at him. "What are you doing?"

"I can ask you the same thing. Don't tell me you're…" He shakes his head. "It's four in the morning, crazy girl."

"Yeah, it's four in the morning." I study him, take a sniff, detecting nothing but Kane's perpetually appetizing, uniquely Kane smell, like fresh air and leather. "I woke up. And you obviously haven't gone to bed yet, psycho boy."

"There was a party. Remember? The one you were invited to and subsequently blew off?" I start to jog away as he calls after me, "I think you made some excuse about having something important to do last night? Whatever it was, I see it allowed you to get up all bright-eyed and bushy-tailed."

I stop. Nothing makes me bright-eyed anymore. Nothing. I whirl around. "You're the one who says I need to do something other than mope. Well, I'm running."

At least I try to. I never ran track in high school, but I used to run before that for the fun of it. These days, I can't remember what fun feels like. I run to escape. It's not fun. It's a matter of life and death.

"You didn't stretch good enough. You'll get shin splints."

"Thank you, coach," I growl at him.

He holds up his hands, acquiescing. I think he's going to leave me alone, but then he comes up close to me. Too close. He reaches up and plucks the earbud from my hand, putting it against his ear. "Good song."

Kane hates this band. "You're smashed," I tell him.

He shrugs. "Maybe."

"Where's Luisa?"

His playful look dissolves. "Why do you always ask me about her?"

"She's your girlfriend."

"Right." He drops the earbud and starts to walk away. Sighing, I stick it in my ear and continue out of the cul-de-sac, breaking into my normal run.

I did cross-country in middle school, but always ended up near the end of the pack. Even though my runs now are not timed, I feel like I'm faster. But it doesn't matter how fast I am. Some things you can't run from. Besides, I'm going in a circle. Brookline Way, the main road of our development, is a three-mile loop, so the jog to my front door makes for a perfect 5K. I used to be out of breath running the mile around the track in gym. Now I can loop around like a washing machine, over and over again until I lose count. The only thing telling me to stop is the sun creeping over the horizon.

I've passed the first few houses when I feel like I'm being followed. I shake the water from my brow and glance behind me as he comes barreling up to my heels. I pull out my earbuds and groan, "I thought you were going to mug me."

"You shouldn't be jogging alone," he says.

"I jog nearly every morning."

He falls in pace with me. Ever the athlete, even drunk, Kane can beat most anybody. He surges ahead of me. I'm going too slowly for him. He's wearing his running shoes. He must've gone in and changed. "Not a good idea. You'll break your neck on some ice."

"Maybe."

"What? And that would make you happy? This self-destructive behavior shit is getting really old."

"This isn't self-destructive! *You're* the one running with me after a night of hard drinking." I scowl. "Leave me alone, Kane."

We've already gone about a quarter of the loop. I know I can't lose him, so I stop. He runs a few paces, then slows, bending over. Finally, he looks a little beat. As much as I love Kane, I have to admit I'm glad whenever I see a rare chink in his armor.

He inhales deeply, braces his lower back with his hands. "Oh shit. I might puke."

I roll my eyes, then start to jog away. "Goodbye, Kane."

"Hold up, Hail. Just hold it," he begs. When he uses that tone of voice, I have a hard time not doing what he says. I slow. He comes up to me and says, "There's another party. Next weekend. It's at Luisa's. Her parents are out of town, and Erich's home from college. He's bringing the beer. And she really wants you there."

"Sure she does."

"No, she does. She wants things to go back the way they were. We all do."

"They can't."

"Okay, they can't. But maybe we can strive for, you know, hanging out with your friends?"

I open my mouth, but what I'm thinking—that I'm not sure these people are my friends anymore—doesn't come out.

"He would want that. You know he would."

I hate how everyone professes to know what *he* would want. Because I thought I knew him best, and yet I clearly had no clue. From what I know of Declan, if you asked me what he wanted most, I'd say *to be alive*.

Still, me not moving on was not because I thought Declan wanted me to lie down and die with him. That's all my choice. "All right," I tell him.

He smiles. Then Kane steps close to me, close enough so that his face is all I can see. Is he going to kiss me? I can't... I won't...

Declan was my first kiss. It happened a little more than a year after what I did with Kane. I'd gone into it expecting bad breath, slobber, and teeth clattering against each other. Instead, it was an experience so memorable that I can still taste him on my tongue every morning when I wake. I can still feel the pressure of his finger under my chin, drawing my lips up to meet his mouth.

Declan was also the last person I've kissed. And I'm not ready for the taste of him to go away.

Something in Kane's eyes tells me he knows it. He pushes a stray lock of hair behind my ear, then walks to the side of the road, leans over a pair of scrubby evergreen bushes, and vomits. I think about rubbing his back, telling him it's okay, but before I can, he wipes his chin and jogs off toward home, arms over his head like a triumphant prizefighter, as if nothing in the world can touch him.

352 Days Before

"Come on, Hail," Declan said as he settled his strong hands around my waist and lifted me up the climbing wall to the top of the playhouse. "This is going to be incredible."

I shivered as I scooted into the playhouse and pulled the blanket I'd brought up to my shoulders. He'd set up what looked like a telescope, sort of. It was made with a cereal box and an old Eight O'Clock coffee can and some other household items. That was Declan. He'd work on his car with his stepfather, but then get these brilliant ideas and build gadgets in his room too. Those gentle Californian hands of his never sat idle.

"I thought they said we could see this with the naked eye."

It was a cold and silent February night. He fussed with his contraption as I pulled the furry blanket tighter over my shivering shoulders. "They did, but why see something naked when you could see it clothed?" he murmured, then smacked the side of his head. "Scratch that. Some things I would much rather see naked."

I grinned. "I don't think I want to know what."

Somewhere along the line, all the time I'd been spending with Kane became eclipsed by time spent with Declan. Before long, being alone with Declan felt natural. But there was no denying it was different. The way he looked at me. The way he talked to me.

And he touched me. At first, innocently: a finger on my arm, or holding my hand to guide me somewhere. Now he held my hand all the time. Now my hand expected it, wanted it, wasn't complete without his.

He gazed through the eyepiece, as I stared at the full moon rising in the sky. I could see the objects of this expedition pretty clearly. Small, clear, glowing Venus beside the moon and the red dot above, Mars, in a picture-postcard tableau. I'd never cared much for astronomy, but this was cool.

"Look," he said, motioning me toward the eyepiece. I stooped and squinted at it.

Yep, there they were, the planets, only slightly larger. "It's amazing," I breathed.

He looked up, then slid beside me under the blanket. "I think this piece of crap is pretty useless. It looks better naked."

The moon was full, casting light onto the icy water in the

retention basin. Our breath puffed out in white clouds in front of us. "Well," I acknowledged, "some things do."

He turned toward me, pulled the blanket up around our ears, and I felt the pad of his finger under my chin, lifting my face toward his. He kissed me lightly on the lips. His lips were surprisingly warm. I'd expected drool and other gross stuff, but this was anything but gross. My lips parted, wanting more.

He said, "Have you never done that before?"

I blushed. "It's obvious?"

He laughed softly. "No. But you looked surprised. Like you didn't expect it."

"I'm surprised I enjoyed it so much."

He looked confused. "You thought kissing me would be disgusting?"

"No," I backpedaled, blushing more. "I... Forget it. You can do it again."

He didn't have to be asked twice. He leaned in and kissed me, still gently, but with tongue this time. Eventually all those shivers went away, and it was entirely too warm. He lowered me back on the wooden floor of the playhouse as we each grew bolder and the kiss became deeper. We started to feed on each other's lips until I was pretty sure we'd tear them clean off.

But we didn't do anything else. His hands stayed firmly on my shoulders. Every so often he'd pull away and trace a line down my cheek, or look into my eyes. But he concentrated solely on my lips.

After a while, I pointed to his watch. "What time is it? I'd better go in."

He shrugged.

Punching him, I grabbed his wrist and thrust the watch into the moonlight. I could barely read it because the face was badly scratched. It said something like 3:15. Kissing him had been magical, but I didn't think I'd lost complete track of time. Then I saw the second hand wasn't moving. "Your battery's dead."

"Hasn't worked since I put it on. It's my dad's. He had it on when he..."

Declan cleared his throat, and it sounded as though he was trying to choke back a sob. His body was tense. The butterflies that had been fluttering in my stomach became cinder blocks. Before, I'd never thought much about how his father had died. Yet I really wanted to know. "Was he sick?"

"Car accident." The words were so soft it was as if he'd traveled to a faraway planet. Long moments passed before he squeezed my hand.

Right. His faith had gotten him through. I guessed that if his dad hadn't died in a car accident when Declan was thirteen, his mom never would've been on the internet looking for companionship. And Declan and I never would've met.

It was his death that made this moment possible. Beauty from suffering.

When I realized that, I figured my parents could wait a little longer. I lifted my head and kissed him again, drawing him down to me.

I'd known Declan for a year. He had a way of walking, loping about, that made him never seem to be in a hurry. When he hovered over a new model, he worked calmly and deliberately. I knew he'd take things slow with me.

But that night, I wanted to speed everything up. It's the feeling I think you can only get when you know that you're finally headed in the right direction.

Tuesday, February 19

I wonder if therapists wait for their patients to leave, then pull a bottle of whiskey from some hidden stash and go to town.

I've been with Juliet every other Tuesday morning, before school, for nearly five months. Before that, when I lived at Shady Harbor, it was *every* day. I've told her the same things a thousand times. It's been eleven months of her asking me the same questions, offering me validation for feeling the way I do, gently suggesting ways I might break through whatever's bothering me. She's been making suggestions for forever, but I've never actually stepped up and done what she said. Every time I see her, I think she's disappointed in me.

"Do you think I'm in a rut?" I ask her, sitting in her plush office. She has about twelve mismatched chairs gathered around this enormous, rust-colored shag rug, possibly because crazy people are picky, like Goldilocks. If a chair is too hard or too soft, they might not adequately pour out their souls.

She looks at me over the top rim of her glasses. "Do you think you might be?"

Her old standby: answering a question with a question. Sometimes I wonder why we pay her, since she always makes me solve my own problems.

"Because, I mean, his own mom has cleaned out his room. Everyone has moved on but me."

Juliet smiles. She's slight and kind of pinch-faced, so even her smile has a way of looking feline, as if calculating my demise. I've never felt one hundred percent comfortable with her, but that didn't stop me from spilling my guts. She knows everything about me. Everything. "Some people simply take longer to grieve. There is no script for getting over this type of hurt."

I knew that already. I nod and look over at the enormous, wall-size aquarium. Sometimes it feels as if we're the two clown fish in there. Juliet and I keep going in circles, rehashing everything I know to be real, day after day. None of it has helped. None of it will ever help. It won't bring him back.

Boats against the current, borne back ceaselessly into the past...

"Are you still having eating issues?"

I nod. "They've gotten worse. Kane thinks I've gotten worse."

"Well, that was to be expected with the anniversary." She writes something on a legal pad. "How's Kane?"

"He's fine. He's always been fine. That's Kane."

"You sound bitter."

"I am. I'm infuriated, actually. I wish I could turn off my emotions that easily. Tune out the way he does. Of course, he wasn't as close to Declan as I was."

"You are very close to Kane, though."

"Not as close as I was to Declan."

"You ever think Kane was jealous of that? Of you and Declan?"

"What, you mean...? No, Kane has no interest in me in that way. He has a girlfriend. Lots of girlfriends."

She nods, writes something else. Every time she makes a note, I can't help but think I said something wrong. "Are *you* jealous of that? Because Kane has moved on after your relationship and wasn't there to pick up the pieces after Declan died?"

"What relationship?" I mumble. "He convinced me to have sex with him once, when I was young and stupid. That's all."

"Did you need that much convincing?"

"What?"

"What I mean is, were you hoping then that it would be more?"

"No. Of course not."

More scribbling. I don't think she believes me. "That was your first sexual experience, yes?"

I nod. "My only. Declan and I never... I mean...it never happened."

"Tell me about last week."

I cross my arms defensively. "Yeah, the anniversary was hard. Then Declan's mom gave me a box of his things. She thought I wanted them."

"And you didn't?"

I unscrew a Poland Spring bottle and take a sip of water. "No. I put it under my bed." I swallow. "And then she gave me this picture. It started me thinking. I've been going over his death in my mind again and again. For so long, I felt like I was the only one who knew the real Declan. Except he kept secrets from me. Maybe that's the reason I haven't been able to move on—because he's been begging me to solve the mystery of his death from his grave."

She straightens. "Declan killed himself, Hailey."

I nod. Whoops. That was a little too *Masterpiece Mystery* for therapy hour. Best not to test my out-there theories with a lady who has the authority to commit people to the nearest mental ward. "Yes. I mean, obviously. But I still don't know *why*."

She presses her lips together. "You don't?"

I shake my head. "Everything's so twisted in my head. I can't remember a lot. Details come to me randomly. As if someone ripped up my past and scattered the pieces in the air."

"We discussed this. That's called selective retention. It's a perfectly normal coping mechanism of someone with dissociative personality disorder brought on by trauma. Your brain is simply not willing to process memories it might find uncomfortable, so it ignores them."

"Yeah. Like what th—" I stop. *Things that I might find uncomfortable.* Bad things, obviously. "I want to remember it all. So I can…" *Solve the mystery of his death? He's begging me from the grave to do so! Nice try, Sherlock.* I shrug. "So I can understand why. I think if I know why, I'll be able to move on."

She pulls out her file and starts to read back a few pages. "It says here you did know why. You thought it was stress."

"I don't believe that anymore. Maybe that's what bothered me. It never seemed right. He was excited about college, not stressed. And he…he was really religious. I mean, don't suicides go to Hell in Catholicism? He totally believed all that. He never would've done it. Never, even if he was under stress."

She rereads the file, nodding. "You said a few sessions ago that you never saw any signs at all. He wasn't sad. Didn't give away belongings. Didn't cut off friends or family."

"Exactly. None of that. He was totally happy."

"Sometimes people can put on very good masks, though."

"Not Declan. Not around me," I say shortly, giving her a scowl. "He had no reason to hide anything from me, and I never thought, even once, that's what he was doing."

"But…you say you don't remember a lot of details. Is it possible you might be—"

"No." I say it with such force that I surprise myself.

She makes more notes. I can tell she's doubtful. "Why don't you tell me about the last time you saw him."

I nod, but very little comes to me. I remember being at his house. I remember the snowstorm was coming and he'd had to get gas. I remember waiting for him to get back. And then… "I don't know. It's hard to… I can't. It was all very normal, though. He wasn't upset. I'm sure of it."

Juliet likes to think she knows Declan. But what I've shared over a thousand hours of therapy can't paint a full picture of him. Declan may have had only one mode—happy—but it was of a thousand different colors, like a rainbow, each hue different and beautiful in its own way.

"What was that you said, about a picture?" she asks.

I blink. Hadn't I already explained it to her? "Oh. Yeah. It was shady. It felt like, I don't know, something that couldn't have belonged to Declan. It was a picture of bodies, too blown up to see everything, and it said, THIS ENDS HERE."

"Can I see this picture?"

"No." I flash back to Kane ripping it up and sigh. "That's another thing. Kane tore it up, and I got the feeling he isn't being totally honest with me, either. I think maybe he got Declan in the middle of something. Declan was probably trying to help him sort it out, and…"

I trail off when I realize I'm babbling. Juliet is staring at me as though I've gone off the rails again.

"If he was trying to help out Kane, that doesn't offer an explanation as to why he killed himself, does it?"

The words sit there, on the tip of my tongue, waiting to come out. In my mind, I see Juliet's finger hovering over a red "commit" button, ready to press it.

He didn't kill himself.

He didn't, he didn't, he didn't.

"No," I mumble. "But I still think there's something wrong with this picture."

She studies me for a long moment. Then she says, "Let me ask you something. If you want to remember, why did you hide the box under your bed? Go through it. It won't be easy, but maybe your heart is strong enough to withstand the memories. It might be therapeutic and give you the answers you're looking for."

I stare at my hands, fingers laced together on my lap. Usually I toss her suggestions out the window before they finish leaving her mouth, but this time, I play the recommendation over and over again in my head.

Maybe.

Maybe that's what I need to do.

256 Days Before

I had it in my head. Me, coming downstairs on prom night, my parents and my adoring boyfriend gazing up at me, thinking they'd never seen anyone so beautiful.

That didn't exactly happen.

After painting my toenails, I'd accidentally lost my balance while hobbling to the bathroom and twisted my ankle in the hallway. I collapsed like a house of cards, the pain shooting its way up my calf. I also smudged the heck out of my pedicure; there were rug fibers stuck to my red toenails. The zipper on the side of my dress got stuck and wouldn't go up no matter how much I pulled, so with one final yank, I ended up ripping it from hip to underarm. And I hadn't gotten any better at applying eye makeup.

So there I was, raccoon girl, hobbling down the staircase with a safety-pin-closed dress, a flubbed pedicure, feeling all hot and sweaty and like the night I'd dreamed of was ruined.

Then I saw Declan in his tuxedo. He was always a hottie, but that night, he looked debonair, the bow tie accentuating his warm brown eyes and luscious full lips. Even though it was a rental, he owned that tux. James Bond couldn't have worn it better.

And you know what he said?

He leaned into my ear as my mother snapped a photo and murmured, "I've never seen anyone so beautiful."

After that, all my stress and worry melted away. He offered me his arm and walked me down the driveway to the most immaculate old truck I've ever seen. It was gleaming red and seemingly had appeared out of nowhere to be parked in front of his house. My mouth dropped as I realized that was the vehicle that had been under the tarp all this time. I said, "Is this what you've been working on with Mr. Weeks?"

He nodded. "Yeah. It's my grandfather's '51 Chevy. I figure this is a special occasion, so we ride in style. Do you like it?"

He asked as if he didn't know the answer, as if it wasn't already written all over my face. "Oh my God. Yeah."

He tossed the keys in the air and caught them. "Technically, it's my mom's car until I turn eighteen. She's letting me drive it tonight." Then he jogged over to the passenger side, pulled open the door, and bowed with great flourish. "My lady."

Still shaking my head in wonder, I stepped into the pristine cab. It smelled like pine needles, and the leather was shiny white. "What about Kane?" I asked.

Kane had complained like a girl that we were going to have fun without him at Declan's junior prom. So he managed to get Ella Butler, a cheerleader from the junior class, to ask him. He'd casually said that it was a "friend thing," that he was using her for the junior prom ticket, but that didn't mean there weren't rumors swirling around school about him doing Ella too. Kane never could escape that kind of rumor.

Knowing Kane, they were probably true.

Up until then, he'd been flirting hard-core with Luisa, so needless to say, Luisa was crushed by those rumors. But Kane went along as if he was doing nothing wrong, as if he was above the controversy. That's Kane.

"Ella and her girls rented a limo," Declan said as I reached over my shoulder for the seat belt. Before I could, he pulled it across my dress, careful not to destroy the corsage, and clicked it for me. Then he gave me a kiss that made my insides tingle, that made me feel precious, safe.

After he slammed my door, I pulled open the glove compartment and found nothing other than the registration papers and a Bible. This one was filled with sticky notes. He slid into the driver's seat and took it from my hands.

"Sorry if I've been out of it lately," he said, thumbing through the pages.

I hadn't noticed. Declan was Declan. He was always happy. "Oh, it's—"

"Things get jumbled in my head sometimes. At the moment, my feminist beliefs are at odds with my religious ones," he said, tapping the worn leather cover. "Like, I think women shouldn't be equal. I think they should be on pedestals. But sometimes the Bible talks about honoring your husband and I'm like, eff that, it works both ways." He picked up the Bible and showed me a few of the sticky notes. "So I mark the passages I want to talk to Father Brady about. For further clarification."

"You…read the Bible?" I blubbered. I'd never read the Bible. To me, the whole thing needed major clarification because it might as well have been written in another language. "And talk to Father? Voluntarily?"

He nodded as he put the Bible back into the glove compartment and the key in the ignition. "Come on, Hail. He puts his pants on one leg at a time, just like anyone else."

We'd been sort of "together" for a couple months, hanging out in the backyard, looking at stars or swinging on the swings. But this was the first event that could qualify as an actual date. He talked about his faith as if I was his equal, and I usually nodded along, not knowing what to say. I'd been born Catholic and had gone through the sacraments, but it didn't mean I wanted to have a stirring discussion about Jesus. Hell, no. So I told him once that religion wasn't a big deal to me. He smiled and said, "That's okay. As long as you don't mind that it *is* a big deal to me."

"I know." I'd pieced the story together. He'd been kind of like me for years. His father was the religious one. And then his dad died. He and his mom went though some rough months. Then they started going to church more. He hadn't said as much, but it was clear that whatever support he'd gotten from Jesus had saved them. How could I dis anything that had such a positive influence on him?

It wasn't bad. He didn't talk about religion unless somehow it was brought up, and he never pushed me. But he managed to get me to church a lot more. I'd go with him and his mother, and gradually I learned all the prayers and hymns so I wouldn't look like a fool around him. And whatever his beliefs were, no one could deny that he was a fine product. Where Kane was always a little sneaky and devious, Declan would go out of his way to help people, just because.

When we got to the Renaissance Hyatt, where the prom was, he cut the engine and looked at me. "You look like you'd rather die than go in there."

I nodded. It wasn't only those safety pins that were keeping my dress from puddling on the ground, or that my ankle felt like a sausage wrapped in an Ace bandage. I liked hanging out in the playhouse. I liked doing homework on his bed. I liked huddling on the curb next to him as we watched Kane shoot hoops. Somewhere along the line, I'd stopped being social. It was so much easier, the two of us.

Declan leaned over and kissed me on the cheek, then said, "I told you there'd be a surprise, right?" He motioned to the front of the hotel, which was ablaze with lights. Extravagantly dressed bodies were hurrying to the revolving doors, disappearing inside. "It's in there."

I nodded nervously. I knew what it was. It was tradition for couples to rent hotel rooms for the night. They'd tell their parents it was a "group thing," but it wasn't really. All the girls were talking about it. Many of them were holding out to be stripped of their virginity tonight, because nothing says romance like losing it on the same night as ten dozen other girls. A guy would always get the room on the sly, then present his date with the key card as a "surprise." I don't know when it became a tradition, but despite being one of the more suck-tastic Deer Hills High traditions out there, it had nearly overshadowed the whole prom event.

"Okay." I pulled open the door and tottered out, but before my injured foot could find the pavement, he was there. He scooped me up into his arms, bumped the door closed with his elbow, and carried me across the parking lot. I forced a smile. "My hero."

Embarrassingly enough, everyone turned as we approached. People cheered at our grand entrance. When we were inside the lush lobby, Declan set me down and bowed shyly. "Are you all right to walk?" he asked me.

I nodded. These were not my people—they were all a year older, so I barely knew them. No way was I causing any more of a scene. I looked around for Kane. "Where do you think he is?"

Declan read my mind. "Hanging from the chandelier, probably."

Right. We headed down to the ballroom, Declan stopping every so often to chat with one of his friends. I hardly knew anyone. I settled down into one of the chairs, Declan next to me. He propped my foot on his knee for a moment. He looked a little nervous. He kept looking up at the stage, where the DJ was spinning loud dance music. Then he leaned in and said, "You'll be okay if I leave for a while?"

I nodded, and he zoomed off in the direction of the lobby. I knew he'd be back in a few minutes with that key card.

Except then the lights dimmed, leaving one bright spotlight on the stage. Suddenly, Declan stepped into the center of it and started strumming his guitar.

I don't know what the song was. Definitely old-time, something from the fifties, maybe, but he added his own little rockabilly spin on it and sang without his eyes leaving mine. Pretty soon, everyone was staring at me, clapping along and smiling.

When it ended, he jumped from the stage, slid over to me on his knees, grabbed my hands, and gave me a kiss. Everyone cheered.

My jaw was resting on the floor. My first attempts at speaking failed. Finally, as people started to peel their eyes away from us and the applause subsided, I whispered, *"That* was your surprise?"

After that, I relaxed. My ankle felt better too, so we managed to dance. The food was good, and his friends were silly. Kane never showed up, but I managed to talk to a bunch of girls who didn't make me feel like the outsider. When the party started to wind down, Declan took me to the revolving doors, and I wavered on my feet. "Um…" I started.

But it was midnight. The party was over, and we were going home. Like any good boy and girl were supposed to do.

Maybe I'd been caught up in the moment. Maybe it was the way he sang to me. But I didn't want to leave. I watched the others, maybe a little wistfully, hitting the up button for the elevator.

Declan was oblivious. When we got to the truck, he opened the passenger side door and I climbed in. When he kissed me and fastened my seat belt, he asked, "Something wrong?"

"No, I…" I couldn't tell him. "Nothing."

"You look like it's something," he said as he climbed in next to me.

"Are we going home?" I asked.

He rested his hands on his thighs. "Why? Do you want to go somewhere else?"

I shrugged.

He started up the truck and pulled out, then turned onto the road leading us toward home. I said, "Weird we didn't see Kane there."

He laughed. "You mean, *not* weird, knowing Kane."

I tittered along with him. "Did you see that? A lot of people were doing that. Getting rooms, I mean."

He nodded. Then he strained to see out the window. "What way you think is fastest? Route 1 or the turnpike?"

"Oh." I had no idea. I tried to look like I was helping. "I don't know. Go Route 1. No tolls."

He pulled onto Route 1. "Yeah. There won't be traffic this time of night anyway."

I decided to try again. "My parents aren't expecting me home until later. I told them people stay out all night. So we could do something. I mean, I told them I would be with you, so they said all I'd have to do is text."

He looked at me. "Well, what's open now? You want to go to the diner?"

I was perfectly sated by the dry chicken française and stringy green beans with almonds. I shook my head but shrugged, as I hadn't an idea in my mind that didn't involve the hotel.

We ended up at this dead-end road some kids go to that overlooks the reservoir. It's all trees, and the living sounds of the forest come up close to you so that they're nearly inside your head. You can watch the lights of the airplanes landing at the airport across the way, the control tower in the distance. In the moonlight, the water looked like a knife of fine silver.

He said, "I know what you were thinking."

I looked at him.

"I figured you probably already knew," he said, wrapping his long fingers around the steering wheel. "I'm waiting for marriage. I want to find the person I want to spend the rest of my life with. So you don't have to worry."

I blinked. "Oh. I..."

"It feels like you could be that person." He reached over and took my hand. "I've never felt this way about anyone, Hail."

I leaned back in the leather seat, making it rip out an unlady-like squeak. I cringed.

"I want our first time to be really special. Not something we do because Deer High tradition says so." He smiled. "That's stupid."

My stomach dropped. *Our* first time.

Maybe he meant the first time for him and me together.

But I didn't think that.

All I saw was me. The sinner. A sin that grew and spread with every second that ticked by without me setting the record straight.

I nodded. "Yeah. Of course. Right," I said shortly.

He looked up at the dark sky for a moment, at a streak of red making its way to the runway. My hand had gone cold in his. I pulled it away and pointed my eyes to the passenger's side window, pretending to be interested in something in the darkness. I hated that I could see his reflection in the glass.

I waited a few minutes, trying to make it seem like I was fine and dandy, never better. But fifteen minutes later, when he asked me what I wanted to do next, I told him I was tired and ready to go home.

Saturday, February 23

The cheap beer is plentiful, the music loud, the lights low.

Recipe for disaster.

Kane knows I don't want to be here. I'm not sure if he was expecting the party to be good for me. But it's heading in an unhealthy direction.

Even I can tell that, and I'm not all here.

"What's your name?" Random Guy asks over the earsplitting music. He's one of Luisa's brother Erich's friends, I think, visiting from Penn State. He's cute—through beer goggles, at least.

I shake my head, pretend I can't hear him. He wants to know my name as much as I want to know his. His real motive, from the way he keeps looking down at my boobs, is to get into my pants. I tilt back my head and take another swig of my beer, then lean over and kiss his ear and give him doe eyes, the universal party language for "Let's get out of here."

He obliges. He takes my hand, and we stumble through the sea of bodies in the kitchen, up the mansion's sweeping staircase. For a second I forget where I am, but then I see a picture on the wall of Luisa and Kane in their junior prom best. Sure, she wants me here. Kane is so full of bullshit. The second she saw me, she walked in the other direction and hasn't glanced at me since. Kane might have come over to say hi, if it weren't for Luisa constantly corralling him. Javier and Nina didn't show, so I've spent the night drinking, then playing Asshole with a bunch of Erich's friends. After that, the night gets hazy.

As we stagger up the stairs, Random Guy's behind me. I have a hard time believing he only has two hands, because he's all over my front, like octopus tentacles. When we get to the landing, I remember which door used to be the guest bedroom and pull him in there. I laugh as I kiss him, and these are truly sloppy kisses, the way I thought kisses were before I knew better. But I don't care. I don't care that he tastes like cigarettes and his tongue is like a bulldozer trying to excavate my mouth. To show him I mean business, I pull his shirt out of his pants before he can even get the door closed.

His eyes widen. I don't think he expected so much from the quiet high school senior.

But I'm probably not like any quiet high school senior he's ever met.

When we come downstairs, the party is winding down. Luisa is sitting at the dining room table, glued to Kane's side. His eyes rise to meet mine. He puts his beer down and starts to get up. I take Random Guy by the hand and lead him outside into the frigid night.

"It's balls cold out here," he mutters when I plop on the porch swing, sitting on my hands. I motion for him to sit next to me, tell him I'll keep him warm, when he says, "I need another beer."

Then he gets up and leaves me alone.

Not that it matters. He was boring company anyway.

I contemplate how long it'll take to walk home. Luisa lives on the other side of town. Probably five miles. I left my coat inside, but I feel warm enough.

I'm game.

I start to push off the swing as the screen door opens and Kane steps out. "Not so fast."

I sigh. "Leave me alone, Kane. If you're not with me, you're against me. And I am happy the way I am."

"So who is this new you? Because I'm pretty sure I saw the new-and-improved Hailey making out with at least three different guys in there."

I stare at him. I thought they were all the same guy. Not that it matters. "I never said I was improved."

He breathes out. "So what? I saw you pulling that loser upstairs. You fuck him?"

I glare at him. "Not that it's any of your business, but what did you think would happen when you invited me here? That I'd fit back in with these people again? It's not happening. I'm *Mental Girl*. I can't sit around Luisa and smile while she discusses her complexion woes at length as if they matter. I don't care who's doing who or what the latest gossip is. It's all so trivial, it makes me want to rip my ears off."

He buries his hands in the pockets of his coat and looks up at the icicles descending from the storm drain.

"I'm going home," I say.

"Walking? No way."

"I have legs. Why not?"

His hand latches on to my elbow. He shakes his head, then peels off his pea coat and drops it on my shoulders. "You seem to think I didn't care. That this is easy for me," he says more softly. "That's far from the truth, Hail. I'm not against you. You're not alone, all right? You're not the only one who was close to him."

"I feel like I am," I mutter, slumping back onto the swing. "Otherwise, you would know it too."

He sits next to me, making the swing rock. "Know what?"

"That this is all wrong. All this time, I've felt like he was in my head, whispering to me to look closer. But it wasn't until your mom gave me that picture that I knew for sure."

He closes his eyes.

"You're hiding something from me."

He stands quickly, exhaling heavily, then leans against the railing and crosses his arms. "Yeah, I am."

"Who are you protecting?"

"Jesus, Hail!" He shakes his head and stares down at the ground for a long time. Then he mumbles, "That picture was nothing. I'd cheated, okay? On Luisa. And some crazy girl was trying to get me to pay for it."

I stare at him, my mouth open slightly. "That didn't look like your skin. It looked like Declan's. And how did—"

He looks back at the door, as if he expects Luisa to come through it at any moment. "It *was* me," he says under his breath. "And you know Declan. Always trying to make peace. He thought he could help diffuse the situation."

I nod slowly, testing out the theory. *It's a lie.* I know that with certainty. One thing Declan and I both lived for was discussing Kane's romantic pursuits. His love life was like a train wreck. *Declan would've told me about this.*

Kane rubs his arms through his sweater and breathes out a white cloud. "Can you drop it now?"

I start to nod, because I know that's what he wants. Suddenly, the door flies open and Luisa appears behind the screen, silhouetted in the warm orange light from inside. "Oh, there you are," she says sweetly to Kane. I can't see her features, but in the ensuing silence, the already frigid temperature drops another ten degrees.

Kane whirls, and his stony face transforms into an appeasing smile. "Just needed some fresh air."

If her eyes were claws, they would've ripped me to pieces. Starting to close the door, she says, her voice still sweet but clipped with frustration, "This party can't spill outside. I have neighbors who will complain."

Sure, she wanted me here.

Kane gives me apologetic look, then starts to go inside, his eyes beckoning me to follow him. I start to when I catch a look on his face. Fear? Anger? Something in between.

It tells me all I need to know.

Whatever he won't tell me, Declan died because of it.

193 Days Before

I didn't think I could change Declan. I didn't want to.

Well, most of the time.

Declan's room was at the front of the house, overlooking the overhang for the porch. In the Fox Court domino-house floor plan, his room was the same as mine. But because the Weeks family had a rose trellis, I could climb up and meet him outside his window, where we'd crawl up to the roof. If you were really feeling adventurous, you could climb to the back of the house, where Kane's room was, but I never did that, because I valued my own neck too much.

Sometimes, when his mom and stepdad were gone, and we had the house to ourselves, we'd go into his room and wrestle under the sheets. Wrestling was his way of copping feels in places he considered off-limits. I knew he liked it. I knew from the way his hands would hesitate and he'd let out a groan, and from the way his erection pressed against me. When things got too heavy, he'd pull off the covers, scoot to the edge of the bed, and pick up his guitar.

Hair wild and snapping with static, he'd play me a song until he got lost in the music. But I didn't have it bad for music the way he did. I had it bad for *him*. Him, and nothing else. He was my *thing*. And the way he looked there, with his face flushed and his shirt undone, just made me want him more.

I'd fan my face, take deep, measured breaths, but the second the song stopped, I wanted him more than ever. His skin against me. His mouth on mine. I wanted all of him.

He set his guitar down and climbed back toward me, pinning my arms over my head and kissing me.

This. Was. Maddening. What was virginity, anyway? Just a stupid social construct that meant nothing in the grand scheme of things. Sex was good, natural. Not having my virginity didn't make me any less worthy of him. But I hated feeling like it meant everything to him, like if he knew what I'd done with Kane, he'd hate me. I tensed and closed my eyes.

"What?" Declan asked, blinking in surprise.

"I don't know if I can take this much more," I said to him. "I mean, if you and I... We could. No one would know. It's just us."

He shook his head. I knew what he was thinking. His God would know.

Forget it. I sat up, straightened my hair, fastened the buttons that had come undone on my blouse. I opened the door to the hallway. I needed air.

Kane's door was closed. He and Luisa had finally stopped dancing around the subject and gotten together. They'd escaped in there an hour ago, which probably meant they were doing what we were not. Sometimes, I'd hear his headboard bang against the wall and think of him on top of her.

Declan cornered me in the hallway and kissed my neck. He stroked my cheek. "You're mad?"

"A little. You're driving me crazy."

"Well, hell. That's the best place to be," he said with a little smirk, the smirk that made it impossible to hate him. All the while, he kept stroking my cheek, contemplating my every feature.

"You know what's going to happen, don't you?" I murmured. "I want to go to school and start a career and get established and then have a lavish wedding with a billion of our closest friends. But we're not going to be able to wait for that. So we're going to get married the second we turn eighteen, while we're poor and stupid. I don't want to get married like that, Dec. All because of God's rule? It doesn't make sense."

His face turned about as sour as it could get, which wasn't very. "It's not stupid, Hail. We can still do everything we want to do. We simply get to do them as man and wife."

Man and wife. I cringed. I was sixteen, and in no way could I imagine myself married in less than two years. *Married* was, like, true adulthood—like, pay your own taxes and stop raiding your parents' refrigerator. "But you're against birth control, right? I don't want to…"

"I've been reading up on it. It's called the rhythm method, and it seems to work," he said. Then he kissed my forehead, tucked a strand of hair behind my head. "You're too good, putting up with me. You could go and find someone else in a second."

"Stop it. You know I don't want anyone else."

He grinned. "But it hardly seems fair. I don't have to *put up* with you. You're perfect. My dream girl."

I smiled. How could I be angry at him? He always knew the right thing to say.

"You look upset, though. What's wrong?"

I'd gotten good at opening up to him. Whenever he talked, I took it for granted that he was telling me every last thing on his mind, no secrets. I knew I could never do the same. There were thoughts in my head that would make him hate me, and whenever I looked upset, it was always because of that. I lied and told him my old standby. "My parents have been screaming at each other all day."

He nodded. It wasn't the first time I'd told him about my parents' bickering. Otherwise, he never would have known. They did a good job of keeping up appearances.

"I wish they'd get divorced," I mumbled.

He didn't say anything, but he didn't have to. He never offered judgment, but I swore sometimes I could see it on his face.

"I mean, they've tried therapy. They've tried everything. They've changed. Grown apart. I look at the pictures of them from when I was a baby, and they don't even look like the same people."

"Why are you arguing with me? I didn't say anything."

"I'm not." I guess my voice had been steadily rising. "I just… People change."

He contemplated this and then reached out, smoothing the wrinkle on my forehead. "Nothing will change with us, Hail. I know that."

My face blazed. I didn't mean to get louder and more defensive. I took a breath. "I walked in on them once. While they were, you know. I was, like, ten."

He straightened my collar. I could nearly see the blush on his face. There was empathy, and then there was Declan's empathy. He could identify with my emotions so deeply that I could see them written on *his* face. "That must have been awkward for all parties involved."

"They didn't even notice," I said, thinking back to that day. "But I'll never forget it. The way my mom looked. She was just lying there, staring at the ceiling with these dead eyes, as if she'd rather be anywhere else. It made me wonder if she *ever* liked it."

"Ah. It made you wonder if *you* would like it. Or if you would be the same as her," he corrected.

I swallowed. He knew me too well. "That's not true. I mean, you touch me, even innocently, and I…" My voice trailed off.

Declan straightened, suddenly acutely interested. "You *what,* exactly?"

I glare at him.

"So if I… I don't know," he said, studying my body. "Did this…?"

He reached out and touched my elbow.

I giggled.

"Or say, if I did this…" He ran a finger down my thigh to my knee.

I nodded. Then I pointed to the field of goose bumps there. "See?"

He looked up and breathed the hair out of his face. "That's sweet. Hell, you make it so hard. In more ways than one."

I pulled him onto me, and we kissed some more, until I could feel just how hard I made it. Finally, I became so frustrated that I said, "There are other things we can do. You know?"

He sighed against me. "Yeah. I know. But that's all…lust. This is love. This is bigger than that."

My spirit sank. "Oh."

He pulled away and looked at me, surprised. "You want to?"

I thought I could see disgust behind his eyes. So I said, "No. I just thought you might."

He pursed his lips together and shook his head. "No. No. I'm good."

Fantastic, I thought bitterly. But then I thought of my mother. I thought of Kane, on top of me. Knowing what I knew of sex, why did I fill so many hours thinking about it?

Speak of the devil. Just then, Kane's door swung open. He was only wearing boxers and unabashedly scratching his crotch. He ambled toward us, to the bathroom door. "As you were, soldiers," he mumbled, yawning.

Declan watched him, then averted his eyes, embarrassed. Sometimes it was hard to believe two people living under the same roof could be so different.

Monday, February 25

Shady Harbor was kind of like preschool. There were people constantly following us around to make sure we showered and ate and wiped ourselves. We'd have assignments each day like, *Draw a picture of you in your favorite place! If you could dream of being anything, what would it be?* Even though I was in the teen ward, and even though I had a tutor to help me with my schoolwork so I wouldn't fall behind, I felt like a toddler. That was good, because even on my best days, my mind was so consumed by Declan that I struggled to find the will to brush my teeth.

"Thinking is what kills us," Juliet had said. "So the trick is filling your time. Fill your time with tasks, even menial ones, and you won't dwell so much on potentially damaging thoughts."

She was right. My first nights there were the longest. They'd stripped the drawstrings out of my sweatpants and taken the razor from my toiletries bag. Left alone, all I'd done was stare up at the ceiling and think of him. I thought of him with such intensity that my retinas might have burned his image on the water-stained ceiling over my bed.

And I wanted to die too.

"You need to make a plan," she'd told me. "Imagine yourself in another year. What do you want to happen? Where do you want to be?"

But I couldn't see myself anywhere without Declan.

Eventually, they got me sewing Christmas stockings for disadvantaged kids during free time. I went to therapy classes where I had to put my thoughts and feelings into artwork. At group, we didn't talk so much about what was bothering us, but about who we were, what we liked, what we were hoping to get back to. I started filling trays with food I liked to eat instead of being force-fed disgusting mac and cheese.

I started to learn how to live for myself. And I started to make that plan. But it didn't really formulate in my mind until I saw that picture. THIS ENDS HERE.

I am better, miles better than I'd been. But it will never be good enough. Not until things are set right. And maybe not even then.

But I should try, right? For Declan, I should try.

"Mrs. Weeks went into labor last night," my father tells me as I come downstairs. "Bill asked me to keep an eye on the house while they're at the hospital."

"Oh," I say. Mr. Weeks never seemed to trust Kane with that. Not that Kane ever burned the house down. If Declan had been around, Mr. Weeks wouldn't have worried for a second. "I'm going to get ready for school."

He laughs. "You haven't looked outside, have you?"

I raise an eyebrow, then stumble to the nearest window. There's a fine blanket of snow on the ground. *Hallelujah.*

"We're supposed to get blizzard conditions later. The weather's calling for two feet."

Hallelujah, even more. That means no school, likely, for the next few days. Excitement wells inside me, which I quickly squelch when I think of Juliet. *The trick is filling your time.*

The plan inside me feels like it's dangling from a very thin string, ready to snap. Exactly what will I fill my time with, cooped up inside for the next few days?

I go up to my room and slide under the covers, wiggling the Cheez-It crumbs between my toes. Then I peek over the side of the bed at the dust ruffle. My heart buckles. Sweat slides down my rib cage.

I'm not actually going to do the one thing guaranteed to make me bawl, am I?

Juliet's voice again: *It might be therapeutic.*

I lift the dust ruffle and root around under the bed, feeling the hard edges of the cardboard box. Taking a deep breath,

I yank back one of the flaps and reach inside. My fingertips come in contact with the rough pages of a book, a marled leather cover.

I know this. There can be nothing more innocent. I pull it out and study the words inked in gold on the front: HOLY BIBLE.

I swallow. This book has been responsible for saving countless lives, right? Why do I feel so unprotected?

He'd kept it in the glove compartment of his truck. He'd carried it around school, unabashed. Sometimes I'd go to his room and see him studying it, yellow highlighter in hand.

Highlighter.

I'd never opened the book before. When I flip it open, the first thing I notice is the lines of fluorescent yellow. Many of them. I knew he'd always relied on these words to solve problems and answer questions both big and small, as if the book were a Magic 8 Ball or something. He'd told me the story of his dad once, while he'd cradled this book in his lap. He'd said the Bible was responsible for saving his life.

My eyes fall upon something highlighted from Corinthians. For some reason, this line is highlighted in bright purple:

"Do you not know that the unrighteous will not inherit the kingdom of God? Do not be deceived; neither the immoral, nor idolaters, nor adulterers, nor sexual perverts, nor thieves, nor the greedy, nor drunkards, nor revilers, nor robbers will inherit the kingdom of God."

My hands are marking the cover with sinner's sweat, a shame considering he'd probably touched this cover a million times. The binding's pristine, and there's not a dog-eared page in sight. *He cared for this as much as he cared for me. Maybe more.*

My hands shake. Forget it. I snap the Bible closed and slide it back under the bed. I change into a thermal shirt and jeans and lace up my boots.

I know exactly what to do.

Outside, I grab the shovel and get started. Who cares if we're expecting two feet more? This is what they call getting ahead of the weather. I can shovel all week, if I have to. It'll be good for me. Fresh air, exertion. This will be great. *Filling my time.*

Each time the snow pummels my face in the icy wind, I only think about how much Declan, gentle Californian soul that he was, used to hate the snow. He was so right. Snow blows. I get the entire driveway done, and all the way around the court sidewalk to the Weeks house, without hardly exerting myself. Snow falls steadily the whole time, so when I turn around, everything is coated in white again.

Do you not know that the unrighteous will not inherit the kingdom of God?

Declan never once preached to anyone. He was conscious of sin, worked hard to avoid it and do good. But he only had these expectations for himself. He never faulted anyone else.

"He felt guilty about something," I find myself whispering as Kane comes outside.

He's wearing an inadequate coat, open, collar pushed up to his ears, once again saying eff you to the weather. He closes his eyes, and the snowflakes land on his eyelashes. "What?"

"Declan. Don't you understand? If he'd had a problem, he would've prayed. What he did is a mortal sin. The worst of the worst. He wouldn't have done it, and you know it."

Kane's fist, the one that's holding his coat closed, is white-knuckled. "Maybe he wasn't as perfect as you remember."

I throw the shovel down. "I don't remember a lot. So what's that supposed to mean?"

For the first time, I notice he's holding two sledding saucers: one his, one Declan's. Not that Declan ever used his. "It means, stop asking me to talk about him. *Please.* Let's go have fun."

I snort. "Remember what happened the last time you wanted me to have fun?"

He grins. "This time, there's no alcohol involved. Come on." He inspects my shoveling job and laughs. "Talk about an exercise in futility."

I follow him, head down, to the retention pond. When we get there, we duck under the fence. When the pond is iced over, the hill sloping down to it is perfect for sledding. It's steep but not breakneck, and once you hit the ice, you can glide and glide for ages, straight over to the tree line on the other side. The two of us used to sled together, then go inside and drink hot cocoa, where Declan would be waiting for us, all warm and snug, reading.

"You're going to be a big brother soon," I say as we survey the hill for a place to push off.

"Yep," he mumbles. He hasn't talked about the baby much. Maybe he feels the way I do: that his parents are trying to replace Declan.

Talk about an exercise in futility.

Kane hands me a saucer. I'm not sure if it's his or Declan's— they were both the same red color with the camouflage pad on the center, and both look fairly new despite the fact that Kane got more use of his. I set it down next to his and drop to kneeling as he does the same. "Ready? One. Two. Three!"

As usual, he pushes hard and ends up halfway down the hill before I even start to pick up speed. He hoots as he hits the ice and starts to glide, leaving a trail in the snow. Somehow, my saucer crosses over and ends up exactly in his wake, following him. I'm flying at a breakneck pace. Everything around me is a blur. My hair is wet and in my face, and I'm numb. Then, suddenly, the weirdest thing happens. I open my mouth and start to shriek.

But I'm not scared. For the first time in so long, my cheek muscles pull into what's got to be a smile, because it hurts so much from lack of use. I'm exhilarated.

Being bigger, Kane coasts to a stop well before the other side of the pond. He crouches, watching me. At first, he's far enough away that I'm not worried about crashing into him. But I'm so surprised to be happy that I lose control. And I'm nearly on top of him before I realize I'm not sure how to stop. He expects me to figure it out, maybe to put out a hand, dig my toes into the ice, or pull back on the rope like they're reins, but I don't. Instead, I catch his shocked expression as he manages to rip his hands out of his pockets to hold me back. I barrel into his feet, and for a second, I'm flying, weightless, before my hands and body come in contact with his wall of a chest, pushing him down flat on his back.

Then I'm on top of him. Breathless, laughing.

His astonishment at seeing me this way transforms to some other emotion, which I can't make out through my joy. I only realize his arms are around me when I feel the pressure of his hands, pulling my face toward him. He kisses me.

And I kiss him.

Alive. Finally, I feel alive.

I'm not sure how it happens. One moment, we're kissing in the center of the retention pond. The next moment, the sleds are abandoned, and we're in his foyer. Cold and warm, numb and buzzing—I feel everything at once. He hasn't let go of my hand. He's still kissing me, but now he's pulling off my coat. I push his from his shoulders to the floor, then raise his shirt over his head. His skin is red and damp from sweat and snow.

He kisses me again. "You know I've always wanted this," he murmurs.

"I did too," I tell him, because I have to say something in answer.

"You did?"

What? Was that the wrong thing to say?

He pulls away and inspects me, looking for a trace of irony. "Because last time, I mean, I thought…"

Oh, enough with the talking! There was a time, long ago, when I was dying to know what he'd thought about that day, if he'd even remembered it. But now I silence him with an open-mouth kiss, hard, demanding. When his fingers dance noncommittally at the hem of my shirt, I push him off me and yank my thermal shirt over my head, much to his astonishment. Words bubble on my tongue. *Come on, come on.*

I kick aside the piles of clothes and pull him toward the staircase. I won't look up at the bedroom at the end of the hall, even if it has been repainted and redecorated as a nursery. Instead, I go up the stairs backward, drawing him up by his belt buckle. He keeps trying to kiss me, but I don't want to. Not until we're in his bedroom. When we're there, I fall down on his bed, and he's on top of me, kissing my stomach and undoing my jeans. I reach behind my back and unclasp my bra, then toss it to the side.

He peels my jeans off my hips.

Same room. Same boy. And yet, this is *nothing* like my first time.

I look around the room as he fumbles around in his night table for a condom. *I haven't been in here in years*, I think. Or have I? I can't remember. He has so many more trophies that they've metastasized onto every available surface. On the walls, banners for schools he'll never be able to attend without a baseball scholarship, but not much else. Kane wasn't neat, but he was never sentimental. There isn't a trace of his girlfriend here at all.

"What about Luisa?"

He's naked, rolling on the condom. His shoulders slouch slightly. "What about her?" He kneels between my legs, and I know what's coming next. "Maybe everything feels wrong because *this* is right."

I find myself nodding, even though I wouldn't know right if it fell from the sky and bonked me on the head. He knows the look in my eyes. He knows me too well.

"All those times you were with him, in his room. Only a wall separating us. And I thought, *This is all wrong.* Did you feel it? You had to have to felt it too."

He's staring at me, expecting an answer. What the hell is with all this talking? I shouldn't have asked about Luisa. "Yeah. Of course," I lie. Like I can even remember a time when I felt, wanted to feel.

He spreads my legs, comes up close to me, and I feel him at my entrance. He pushes in with enough fierceness to make me gasp.

"Oh yeah," he growls, and from the look on his face, the intensity of his mouth on my lips, I guess he likes it. His hands are tight on my shoulders as he moves against me, his hip bones grinding against mine. "Do you like that?"

"Oh yeah," I repeat, the words muffled by his skin, because the second he's inside me, I know this isn't right, either. All I can think is, *I must look like my mother did.* What if Declan, wherever he is, can see me now?

I stay quiet, trying to fight back the tears in my eyes.

I've imagined Kane as a lover a million times since what happened between us, and each time, he always does the same thing. He rolls off me, embarrassed, like an awkward fifteen-year-old boy, and we don't talk for what feels like an eternity afterward.

But this Kane doesn't do that. When he's done, he stays inside me, breathing hard, his hand playing near my ear, twisting a lock of my hair. He falls against me, resting his head on my shoulder.

"I love you," he breathes out. Not once. Over and over again.

Why is he getting like this? The great Kane Weeks, why is he getting sentimental *now*? Over this? Over something I started because I wanted to prove to myself I could still feel? I should've cut myself with a file again. It would've been less painful.

I lie there, still, looking over the trophies. He has ones for every year, from when he was in Pee Wees, right on up to last season. I count them, noticing he's missing one from last year. It should be the biggest one, because they'd made regionals. He'd been so proud. But the trophy is gone.

And Kane's still whispering in my ear and twirling my hair around his finger.

Eventually, he realizes I'm waiting for him to get up.

"I never felt like Declan was wrong for me," I say when he rolls off me.

He's sitting on the edge of the bed, laughing bitterly. "Really, Hail? I tell you I love you, and you talk about him? Can you, for one minute, *not* talk about him?"

"I'm sorry," I mumble.

"Really. Was the sex that good with him?"

"I never… We never…"

He's reaching for his pants. He stops and stares at me. "You're kidding me, right?"

I find my bra on the other side of the bed and quickly clasp it. "No. I didn't even do it with that guy at the party." I shrug. "I laughed at him. I called him weak. We're *all* weak…"

"Screw you, Hail."

I scowl back at him.

"Declan wasn't some god. You make him out to be so…" He vises his head in his hands, making his messy hair even messier. "Do you even listen to yourself?"

I swallow.

He sits down on the edge of the bed, so absently he nearly misses it. His voice is quieter. "So…I… You mean, I'm…"

"The only one. Yeah."

He stares at his lap for a long time, at the condom on his shrunken dick. He's hunched and surprisingly fragile. I expect him to say something about how that confirms we're meant for each other. Instead, he mumbles, "So that's what you think of me. That I'm weak?"

He fishes an empty Coke bottle out of his trash bin, peels off the condom, and feeds it in.

"I'm weak too."

When he pulls on his boxers, he snaps, "Compared to Declan? Is that what you were going to say? He *wasn't* strong. You really think that?"

"He had convictions."

He rolls his eyes. "Some convictions. He went against them, Hail. All of them. Remember?"

"No, I don't. What do you mean?"

He throws up a hand. "Well. Obviously. Blowing his fucking head off was against his religion."

I wince. "That's what I'm saying! So you know as well as I do that there's something wrong with this picture. He didn't kill himself."

When it's out in the open, he blinks, a look of profound horror on his face. "Hail. Stop it. Of course he did."

I sigh. "Until I know what happened, I'll always think of him. I can't help it. My mind is a mess, Kane. Juliet calls it selective retention. My mind doesn't know how to process certain memories, so it simply ignores them. But I don't think I can ever get past this until I understand."

He stares at me for a long time, then sucks in a breath. "Wait. Hail. Are you telling me you really don't remember what happened the day he died?"

"I remember some of it. But I don't remember a lot of things, from *weeks* before he died."

He's gaping at me, astonished. "What the hell did they do to you in that place? Shock treatments?"

"A lot of medication." I close my eyes, trying to remember the last time I saw Declan, but the most I can get out is the way he looked at me—the way he always looked at me, as if I was his whole world. Suddenly, though, something comes to me. "He was at home, right? Your parents were away in the Poconos."

Kane nods. He's biting his lip, which means he isn't sure he should tell me something. He says, "So you're not pretending. You really don't remember the weeks before he died? Seriously?"

I nod.

"How many times have we done this?"

"What? You mean..." I point at the condom in the soda bottle. "That?"

We're looking at each other as though we each think the other is crazy. I say, "Twice. Why?"

He smacks his head with the back of his hand. "Holy shit. You seriously don't remember anything."

I swallow. "What are you saying? Care to enlighten me?"

He shakes his head. "Forget it."

How can I forget that? I sit up on his bed, get to kneeling. "Are you saying we had sex before Declan died? That I cheated on him?"

Kane's mouth is a straight line. "Yeah, that's what I'm saying."

What? He has to be lying. I cover my mouth with my hands. "But why? Do you think... Is that why..."

"No. No, Hail," he says, sitting on the bed next to me and taking my wrist, prying my hand from my mouth. "It wasn't. He didn't know about it. But seriously. That's why you need to move forward. Knowing what happened isn't going to help you at all."

Nothing he says penetrates the wall around me. I cheated on Declan. I'm a liar, and a cheater, and...I'm just like Kane.

Kane's somehow managed to get completely dressed, and I'm still sitting in my bra and nothing else. I find my thong inside my jeans and put it on, then stand and shimmy into my jeans. My shirt's still downstairs. I cross my arms in front of my chest. Goose bumps pop out everywhere on my arms. I'm starting to open the door when he grabs me and kisses me. "Just because it wasn't wrong with him doesn't mean it's wrong with me."

"*Nothing's* wrong with you," I mutter. Stupid boy, he's always been glowingly perfect, which has never been clearer to me than now, with him only a hairbreadth away from me, our noses nearly touching. I can't meet his eyes. I make my voice extra tough. "So what does this mean? Are we dating?"

I expect him to say no, but instead his fingers entwine with mine. "Is that what you want?"

No, of course it's not. "I can't do that now. And you have Luisa."

"Forget Luisa." He groans. "You know how I feel about her."

"I know what you tell me. But what you tell her is obviously a different story. She's in love with you, Kane, and you're leading her on."

He digs his hands into the back pockets of his jeans and rocks back and forth on his bare feet, considering this. "Fine. I'll break up with her."

I blink. I don't know why I'm surprised. Kane never got

himself worked up over a girl. Ever. "Don't make this because of me. You owe her that much."

He nods silently, contemplating this, which makes me think I need to explain myself.

"I mean, I don't think I'd be very good at that right now. You know. Dating. Being a girlfriend. Not with…what happened. It's still *way* too soon."

Too soon for…*everything*. Including what we just did.

"Fine. I'll break up with her anyway." When I give him a questioning look, he says, "You're right. Our love-hate relationship is mostly hate. I'm kidding myself. I'll never be happy with her."

Scraping my ragged fingernails against my palms, I tug on the doorknob when I notice something on the top of his dresser, between the neatly arranged trophies. It's a watch. And not any watch. I know it because of the crack on the face, the hands permanently stuck at 3:15. It's Declan's. I pick it up. "Why did you take his watch?"

"I didn't take it. He gave it to me." Kane shrugs. "Actually…he gave it to me the night before he died."

"But this watch was his dad's." He'd loved this thing. I turn it over in my hands. It's one of those fancy diving watches with all the gadgets. I run my finger along the inside of the strap, which had touched Declan's wrist so many times. My breath catches in my throat. I'd told Juliet that Declan hadn't been the typical suicide who gave away his prized possessions. But I was clearly wrong. He simply hadn't given them *to me*. "Did he tell you why?"

Kane shakes his head slowly. Great, another unanswered question to add to the pile. Before I can sigh in desperation, Kane reaches out and tucks a stray lock of hair behind my ear.

I flinch. *Declan didn't know about Kane and me,* I remind myself. Did he? It doesn't matter. Kane is right. I keep trying to find explanations to make myself feel better, and yet, everything I learn makes me feel worse. "I want to go to church," I tell him.

He stiffens, then lets out a breath. "To pray?"

"No. To talk to Father Brady. He and Declan were close. He might be able to share something."

Kane closes his eyes. "Fine. But I'm going with you."

158 Days Before

Labor Day weekend. My father knocked on my door as I was binge-reading *The Great Gatsby*, my summer homework for junior year. The first part of the summer, Declan and I had spent all of our time together. But by August, he'd begun making weird excuses about why he couldn't see me. After that big sex talk, when he'd told me he wanted to wait…something had changed. He stopped coming around and didn't invite me to his room, even when his parents were away. When I climbed up to see him, he was gone, the window locked.

All I could think was that I was losing him.

I'd never been so afraid. So hopeless.

So out of control.

I moped constantly, wondering what I'd done. Had I turned him off somehow? By that last weekend, I checked the calendar and realized that I was well and truly screwed, summer-homework-wise. Most of the stuff I'd been skimming about Daisy and Nick and Jay was bouncing right out of my brain, which was too overcrowded with thoughts of Declan. So by the time my father came in and told me he had something to show me, I was happy for the distraction.

The fact that my dad was at my door was weird enough. When I was a kid, he'd done all the good stuff dads did—carrying me on his shoulders around Disney so I wouldn't have to walk, buying me SpongeBob pops from the ice cream truck, taking twelve hours to set up the outdoor jungle gym so I could play with it for three minutes until I got bored. Now we were virtual strangers without much in common. Weirder still was that he was actually smiling. Usually when my parents were home all day together they were at each other's throats by this time of night.

Holding my copy of *Gatsby* open with my finger to mark the page, I jogged down the stairs after him. He took me to the garage. I thought he was going to show me something out in the driveway—like a nice sunset, or a hot-air balloon, or a turtle he'd found while mowing the lawn—since that's what our interaction boiled down to these days.

It was a bright-red Jeep Wrangler, all shiny and new, with the top down.

All I could think was *boss*. I didn't even know if that was a cool thing to say anymore. I didn't care. The Jeep was boss.

My father and mother stood together, smiling, for once in their lives. "It's yours," my dad said.

My jaw dropped. "Really?"

My mom nodded. "You're going to start your junior year on Tuesday. And we thought you should have your own car, instead of having to take the bus."

Yes. Hell, yes.

I moved closer. On first glance, I'd thought it was new, but as I studied it, I notice little things. A small dent in the front bumper. Scratches in the red paint. A black mark across one of the tan headrests. It was used, for sure. But it didn't matter. It was still boss, and mine. All mine.

I climbed in, still holding *Gatsby*, marveling at all of the mine-ness in front of me. That steering wheel? Mine. Those floor mats? Mine. The dangly little cinnamon-cookie air freshener that hung from the rear-view mirror? Also mine. My mouth wouldn't close; the awe was just too great.

Laying *Gatsby*, open to my page, on the passenger seat, I wrapped my hands tight around the wheel. My father leaned in and handed me a key ring with a shiny key. I slid it into the ignition, then leaned back and stared. "Thank you," I said. Then I noticed the stick shift, and a small part of me deflated. "But I can't drive this."

My mother motioned to the front of the garage. "We've hired an excellent teacher."

I craned to see into the rear-view mirror as Declan came into view. He slid into the passenger's side and leaned his elbows on the half door. "Can I have a ride?"

It all came to me right then. All the time he'd been gone? "Did you…?"

He nodded, opened the door, and slid inside, grinning. Suddenly, all was right with the world, and I had to wonder why I'd been so needlessly mopey for the past month.

He picked up my book. "*Gatsby*, huh? 'So we beat on, boats against the current, borne back ceaselessly into the past.'"

I had no idea what he was talking about. "Did you help with this?"

My father said, "Let's put it this way. A month ago, it was on blocks and hadn't run in ten years."

My jaw dropped. "You fixed it up? Without me knowing? How?"

My father saluted us, and my mother waved. They walked back into the house, leaving us alone. I looked at Declan, wanting to jump him again. He said, "Well, you knew something was up. Tell me you weren't suspicious."

"I was suspicious you'd found a new girlfriend," I said, punching him. I squeezed my hands together in front of me in excitement. Then I leaned over and kissed him on the cheek. "I can't believe this."

"Told you," he said. "We're forever. Now, do you want me to drive, or what?"

We're forever. Of course we were. I found myself smiling, wondering how I could have ever doubted it. Doubted him. I took *Gatsby* from his hands and tossed it into the back seat. "Yes. Let's get out of here."

We spent a couple hours in the parking lot of the Giant supermarket. I caught on pretty quickly. And he made a very attractive teacher, patient, helpful…and all mine. I'd been starved of him for over a month, and right then, it was as if someone had laid a banquet in front of me. About a half hour into the lesson, I couldn't take it anymore. I threw the car in Park, making it squeal.

"Whoa, you want the transmission to drop out of your car?" he asked.

I pushed down the brake, climbed over the stick, and into his lap. "No, I want this." And I kissed him.

He kissed me back, sucking my lower lip into his mouth. "You like your birthday present?"

"Birthday present?" I breathed into his neck. "That was months ago."

I wanted his hands on me, but when I tore my mouth from his skin, I realized he was petting the dashboard. "This sure is a pretty piece of crap you own, isn't it?"

Rolling my eyes, I grabbed his jaw, hard, turning and focusing his eyes on me. Sometimes his car hobby could be a little annoying, as consuming as it was. "*You're* my pretty piece of crap, dude. Kiss me."

He did. But as usual, we stopped before things got too heavy. At least, we physically stopped. As usual, as his erection pressed against my body, my mind stretched out into what *could* happen, if he would only let it. If he would only do what came naturally.

When we got back to the cul-de-sac, it was ten, and I was in a bad mood. For weeks I'd been wanting Declan back, loving me. And now that he was…I wanted more.

I was disappointed, tired, and had made zero progress on that damn *Gatsby* book. As we were pulling into the driveway, my phone lit up with a text. Declan pulled it out of the cup holder and read it. "Luisa."

I groaned. "What does she want?" Luisa and I were still friends. Maybe we weren't the best buddies who hung out all the time and read each other's minds—she had Nina for that—but we were still tight. I looked at the message. **Can I sleep over tonight?**

Luisa hadn't slept over in a year, at least. Oh, she'd told her parents she was sleeping over my house, but most of the time, it was when Kane's parents were away and she was staying over *there*. I always had to cover for her. It was exhausting, doing favors for her, when she never did anything in return. I jabbed in: **Why?**

Then I looked at Declan and sighed. "She wants to sleep over."

He was fiddling with the dials on the center console. "Why do you hate her so much?"

I shrugged. He'd been largely insulated from Luisa, because even though the six of us would always go out, she'd usually only talk to Nina, me, or Kane. Declan really only talked to the boys or me. Luisa's interactions with Declan had been limited.

"You don't know her. She can be a little…much. And she'll probably want to sneak in your window to see Kane."

"I know a little, from what I see when Kane brings her home. She seems nice," he said, casually. "Pretty."

I stared at him. It was an understatement, because Luisa was gorgeous. But what surprised me was that he'd noticed. He'd never, ever given me a reason to think he'd looked at other girls. Now I was more than annoyed. "What?"

"Relax. It's not like I want to do her," he said. No, he didn't want to do anyone, clearly. "I'm human, so I notice these things. Kane treats her like garbage."

"And yet she still keeps going back for more. So whose fault is that?" I asked, dismissing it. I looked at the message that lit up my screen and suddenly felt guilty. **My father had a heart attack, and my mom and brother are spending the night at the hospital with him. I hate being all alone.**

Come over, I typed in, showing the message to Declan. He didn't say anything, but I felt like the bad guy. Kane treated her like garbage, and I can't say I did anything to stop it. No, I encouraged it. But that was what we did, and Luisa didn't ever seem to put up a fight about it. She kept going back for more punishment. "I *hope* she bangs on your window at two in the morning, wanting to see Kane. I can't play nurse to her. I have to write a ten-page report by Tuesday, and I haven't even read twenty pages of this thing."

"*Gatsby*'s good stuff. You'll like it." He shrugged. "Just send her over. He's home."

I was surprised. It wasn't like Kane to be home on a Saturday night. "Doing what?"

He reached into the back seat and pulled out *Gatsby*, which now had a bent cover. "What do you think? Trying to finish up *his* summer homework. You guys are like two peas, you know that?"

I frowned. I may have grown up with Kane, and while I may have loved him, all that made Kane *Kane*—laziness, ego, sarcasm, aloofness—weren't particularly nice traits. I'd have much rather been in that nice, sweet, caring pod with Declan.

But I had to admit, as much as I didn't want to believe it, that he probably had me pegged right.

Tuesday, February 26

I never thought I'd see the day Kane went to church.

It's eleven o'clock on Tuesday. We should be in school, but most of the roads are closed, choked by snow. We haven't gotten the two feet the weather report called for, but we got enough to cancel school and my regular morning appointment with Juliet. She called, wondering if I wanted to Skype, but I told her there was really nothing new to talk about, and I could wait another week. She agreed. She probably thought she was in the clear, since she'd gotten me through February 14 in one piece.

After Kane and I finished shoveling out the cul-de-sac, I threw my Jeep into four-wheel drive and we hit the road.

We're chugging along, slowly making our way through the snow, when he gets the call. It's his dad. He talks to him for a few minutes, saying *uh-huh* a thousand times, in monotone, and then hangs up.

"It's a boy," he says, his tone flat. "They named him Cooper."

"Congrats," I say, though I can tell he isn't in a celebratory mood.

"Cooper the Pooper."

"Nice. You'll be a great big brother."

I intend to be sarcastic, but actually, Kane might be. He doesn't like much, but the few things he decides to love? He throws his whole self into them, and his loyalty is boundless. I could see him taking the kid under his wing.

He doesn't say anything in return. It isn't until we're almost at the church that he finally speaks.

"I don't know what you're expecting to find here," he says to me as I pull into the parking lot. Predictably, it's empty, although a plow's come through.

I park in the first open space after the handicap spaces and shrug. "Maybe Father Brady will tell me more than you're telling me."

He looks up at the white building, and I don't think I've ever seen Kane look quite so out of sorts. "What do you want me to tell you?"

Oh, now that we're in front of a church, he's going to come clean? "*Bzzz*. Too late." I put my hand on the door handle. "I've asked you a dozen times to help me figure out what happened before his death, and you haven't."

He leans back in the passenger seat. "Okay, I'll tell you. I mean, it was nothing earth-shattering. That's why I didn't tell you. I—"

"I thought you'd said we…" *Had sex.* Why can't I bring myself to say it? "You know. That wasn't earth-shattering?"

He sighs. "Do you remember Christmas that year?"

I nod. Our last Christmas, our only Christmas as boyfriend and girlfriend, and I couldn't even celebrate it with Declan. Mr. Weeks had taken the family on some skiing trip, and Declan had texted me about a million times, completely miserable, since he didn't do snow. But before he left, he'd given me a necklace with a tiny diamond in the center of a heart. "Diamonds are forever, and so are we," he'd said solemnly. Then he'd laughed as he put it around my neck. "I read that in a jewelry ad."

The memory pulls tears from my eyes. How did I repay him for that kindness? By cheating on him? It all seemed so cruel of me. I squeeze back the tears. "I do. I even remember the New Year's party. At least the first part of it. We were at your house, right?"

"Yeah. And we all got a little smashed that night, so I can't help you with that," he says. "But after Christmas break, we—"

"Wait. Wait. Wait." I reach into my bag and pull out a little notebook. In it, I'd made a calendar. I'd been filling it in with events as they happened. Memories. "Okay. After break. Go on."

"We got back in January. So, January 2?" He leans back and put his snow boots up on the dashboard. They're covered in salt and sand, but my Jeep is beyond help, so I don't worry. I write:

Jan 2. "You remember that? We all came back to school, and you were worried that Declan was acting weird."

"I was?"

He nods. "You wouldn't tell me what the deal was."

I rack my brain. Had Declan ever acted weird? Well, he normally acted weird, but in a delightful way. Nothing that ever worried me. I shake my head helplessly.

"That week you suggested we go to the movies. So we did. All six of us. Remember that?"

None of this rings a bell. "What did we see?"

"That stupid horror movie. The one about the teens who get stranded in the house on the mountain, and then all of them start to die?" He takes in my blank expression and says, "It's no wonder you don't remember. It was pretty forgettable."

Yeah, but not only do I not remember the movie, I don't remember the entire outing. I scratch my head. On the calendar, it looks like that day would have been January sixth. Five weeks before Declan died. This is good. I finally feel like I'm getting somewhere. I write *Movies with the 6* in the box for that date.

"And everything was good that night?"

He nods. "Wait...no. I think you and Luisa got into it that night?" A cold gust rattles my Jeep, and icy air infiltrates the tattered soft top. He pulls his fleece jacket closed and blows into his hands. "It was more than a year ago. I can't remember everything."

I make a note of that. We fought. Luisa was all sweet sunshine, but when she got pissed, it could get ugly. "I wonder what we fought about."

He looks at me like it's obvious. "Me."

"What?"

"Well, Declan didn't know about you and me. But Luisa always suspected something."

I stare at him, openmouthed. Then I reach forward and smack him upside the head. It doesn't faze him. "If Luisa suspected something, what was to stop her from telling Declan?"

He thinks for a moment. "She wouldn't."

"And why not?"

"Because I'd get pissed at her. And you know she loves the shit out of me."

"Oh my God." That's his reasoning? I stare at him as if he's an alien being. If Luisa told Declan about us… I shiver. I can't even think about it. "You are so fricking full of yourself, it's ridiculous. Come on. You *need* this place."

I pocket my notebook and push open my door. St. Andrew's is on a hill, so the wind always whips right across the parking lot, freezing poor worshippers before they can make it through the doors. "What?" He lingers in the Jeep, but finally gives up and follows me.

"You need church, if only to remind yourself that you're not the bright center of the universe," I mutter.

He follows after me like a recalcitrant child, arms crossed over his ski jacket. We go inside, and when we're in the atrium and I'm uncoiling my scarf from my neck, it hits me. I've been going to this church sporadically since I was a baby, but I've never actually carried on a conversation with Father Brady. Or, really, any religious type. Declan went on and on about him so much, making him seem like a regular guy, but he's not. He's a priest.

He might be able to see through me.

Still, I need to do this.

Pulling my coat around myself as if that will better insulate me from his divine power of sight, I walk down the empty hall toward the church office. There's a light on, and I can hear typing. Real, honest-to-goodness typewriter typing, complete with the bell and zing of the carriage return, slow though it might be. Kane lags behind me, looking up at the pictures on the wall: our bishop, our cardinal, the pope. Kane looks like he's never seen any of them before. I've never actually seen him out of place somewhere, but I guess there's a first time for everything.

He pauses before we reach the door. "You know," he says, pointing away from the office. "I'll wait out here."

I start to argue, but decide I don't need him. "Fine."

I creep to the door, and the second I peek in, someone shouts, "Shit!"

Father Brady rips a page from the typewriter, crumples it into a ball, and tosses it. It bounces off my head and lands at my feet.

He sees me and covers his face with his hands. "Oh dear."

There's a trash can behind me. I bend over, grab the discarded paper, and drop it in. "Um, Father Brady?"

He nods. "I'm sorry. I didn't think anyone was here. My secretary called in sick. Flu. So I'm trying to type out these marriage certificates."

"Oh."

"Do you know how to use one of these?" he asks, feeding a paper into the typewriter. He slumps down in the chair. "Of course you don't. You probably don't even know what a fax machine is."

I shake my head.

Father Brady would've been attractive in his youth. He's probably about forty, with a stomach pooch and a bit of a bald spot. He motions me to sit in the old upholstered chair across from him and stares determinedly at the typewriter. When I perch on the edge of the seat, he says, "And what can I help you with, Miss…"

"Ward," I say. "Hailey Ward."

His eyes snap up, and he regards me again through his bifocals, fingers hovering over the keyboard. "Declan's Hailey?"

I nod, pulling the jacket tighter across my body.

He takes his hands off the keyboard. Removes his glasses and a handkerchief from his pocket, and starts to polish the lenses. Without them, he looks oddly young, like a different person. "I was wondering when you were going to come see me. How are you?"

"I'm fine," I say. "I mean, it's been a year. So I don't need your help. I mean, spiritually. I'm good."

Oh gosh. I'm babbling.

He seems surprised. "I think we could all use God's help, whether or not we think we do."

I nod along. Probably. "What I mean is, there are some things that still puzzle me about his death, and I was wondering if he'd said anything to you that could help shed some light on it. Since you two spoke often."

He nods and pushes his glasses onto his nose. "I have to admit, when I heard the news, I thought it was a mistake. Did you think the same?"

I nod. "Yes. That's why I thought that maybe you had some idea what was troubling him."

He shakes his head. "Not a clue. Nothing that seemed to be troubling him enough to do what he did. He had guilt over his father, of course."

"Over his father?"

"Yes. He felt responsible for his death."

I rack my brain, trying to remember if he ever told me that. No. He'd said he talked to his father. But he'd never said he felt guilty about his death. His father had died in a car accident, on the way home from work. How could he have felt responsible? "He did?"

"Oh yes. That was a major theme of our talks. He was big on guilt. Beat himself up over fear of doing the wrong thing."

Looking back, Declan never seemed to do the wrong thing. I thought he'd always done right effortlessly.

Father Brady lets out a heavy sigh. "Other than that, he had the same troubles as any boy his age. School. Future. Girls."

Girls. Me? He had trouble with me? Oh. The whole sex-before-marriage thing. I'm not going to touch that topic with a ten-foot pole with Father Brady. I stand. "All right. Well, thank you."

"Of course," he says as I put the scarf around my neck. "Declan didn't come to see me at all in the time before he died."

I stop winding my scarf on my neck and stare at him. "What do you mean?"

"He used to come and see me every Tuesday evening, like clockwork," he says, making me think of my own Tuesday appointments with Juliet. "He knew I had a penchant for Big Macs, so he'd always bring me one, and we'd sit and have dinner together and talk about life, maybe play a little chess."

Okay, so that was nothing like my appointments with Juliet. I didn't even know Declan knew how to play chess. "And you say he stopped coming?"

He nods. "The last time I saw him was before Christmas. He didn't show up after that. He even stopped showing up at Sunday masses, though his mother did. When I asked, his mother said that he was fine, that he'd bitten off more than he could chew and was busy with school. The year before college is a busy year, so I didn't think anything of it."

I stare at him, mouth agog. Declan had stopped going to church? I didn't think anything short of a natural disaster or death would keep him from church. "Thank you."

"You're welcome." Father Brady pushes his glasses up to the bridge of his nose, refocusing his eyes on the paper in front of him as I head for the door. Before I can escape, he says, "Your family doesn't come to church anymore. But you used to go with Declan. Did you lose your faith when he died?"

Talk about guilt. I feel it seeping in. "No," I say. I could say more, but I don't.

Instead I leave. Because he wouldn't like the rest: *I never really had any faith.* I wanted it. I thought Declan could give it to me. I'd wanted to be more like him. And yet…that never happened.

He stopped going to church.

He lost his faith.

Something made him lose his faith.

Something, or someone.

I hold my chest as I walk through the empty hallway, the

figures in the stations of the cross staring down at me. I feel like my heart might beat out of my chest.

I find Kane inside the sanctuary, sitting in a pew in the back, looking up at the altar. I nudge him over and sit beside him. "Did you learn anything?"

"Father Brady says he hadn't seen him since Christmas," I whisper, as if the statues surrounding us are listening. "He didn't go to church before his death. For, like, six weeks."

Kane looks down at his lap, and it almost looks like he's praying. "Strange."

"I don't think he'd ever be so busy as to miss church. But I found out why he felt guilty," I say. "His dad. He felt responsible for his death."

Kane nods, unsurprised.

"You knew that?"

"Yeah. His dad was coming home from work, but Declan called to tell him he needed to get picked up from his friend's. His dad reached for the phone while he was driving and lost control of the car."

He never told me that. As close as we were, Declan never told me that. And it wasn't anything he couldn't tell me. I thought I was the closest person to him. It was hard to imagine any two people being closer than him and me.

Until now.

"Oh. He never told me."

"Well, it's not something you bring up in casual conversation."

Casual conversation. Our conversations had long since stopped being casual. In fact, all we did was have deep, meaningful heart-to-hearts. We'd spent so many quiet nights together, telling each other our stories, that when the week before Christmas came around and we went out to Friday's for dinner, we'd sat together staring at our phones, barely talking. I'd been quiet because I couldn't think of anything to say, since there was nothing about me he didn't know. I'd already poured my soul out to him, so there wasn't a single side of me that he hadn't seen. But Declan?

He'd had things to tell me. He just chose not to.

The thought makes my heart ache. I stand, without a word, and go outside. Kane follows a few minutes later, after I've already twisted the key in the ignition. "See," he says, opening the door to the passenger side. "Told you that you'd take this too hard."

"I'm not taking anything hard," I snarl, reaching into my bag and pulling out the notebook. I scan the calendar and say, "What happened on January 7?"

He lets out a laugh. "Well, that was the day I was wearing the red Aeropostale shirt." When I scowl at him, he throws up his hands. "How should I know, Hail? It was a long time ago!"

"It was the day after the movies," I prompt. "Sunday."

He thinks, then hitches a shoulder. "I don't know. Let me think on it. I'll file a full report in the morning, officer."

I ignore the attempt at humor. "When did we have sex? That day?"

He shakes his head. "No. That was later. I don't know the date."

I throw the notebook into the center console and shift out of Park. "Well, think. Please."

"Yes, sir."

"I'm serious." The sun is so bright against the snow that I wish I had my sunglasses. I look over at him and see starbursts. I'm getting a headache. "You will, right?"

He mumbles, "Yeah. Sure."

I don't know if he really means it. I can tell he's getting annoyed with me, but I don't care. I pull out onto the main road and gun it through the slush. My Jeep starts to rattle and whoosh with the wind so I have to yell, "What are you moping about now?"

"I'm pissed that you have absolutely no recollection of our mind-blowing time together, so yeah, I'm moping," he yells back.

I give him an annoyed look. "You know what I've been thinking?"

"About how much you want a repeat performance?"

I cringe. "Can you stop being a total horndog and focus? I was thinking about the shed."

He lets out a sigh. "Right. Of course. Why think of your living boyfriend when you can think of your dead one?"

"Stop. I'm not your girlfriend. What—"

"Because you don't want to be."

I huff. "Let's not talk about that now. Listen. Do you think we can go by the police station? I want to talk to Nina's dad."

Without waiting for an answer, I start heading there. It's around the corner from the church, so it would be a wasted opportunity not to.

"What do you expect he'll tell you?"

"Declan hated going into that shed when he had to mow the lawn. He used to tell me that the chemicals made his eyes water. He avoided it at all costs."

"Yeah, well, apparently he didn't avoid it that day," Kane says, looking out the window. He starts to play with the frayed edge of the soft top.

I'm so deep in thought that I don't come out of it until I find myself sliding on a patch of ice from driving too fast. Overcorrecting, I look at Kane, and he's bracing himself, holding the door handle. "Chill. I've got it."

He loosens his grip. "You know what? Drive us off the road. Kill us. Since you only seem to think about the dead."

"Sorry." I slow down, though I'm dying to get to the police station. I lower my voice from a yell. "And the gun? What about that? Your dad kept his guns under lock and key, didn't he?"

He nods. "Uh-huh. Key was in my father's bedroom, in the top drawer of his dresser."

"Declan didn't care about guns. Did he even know that?"

Kane shrugs. "Guess so."

I don't buy it. Declan was anti-gun, I'm sure. We pull into the parking lot of the police station, between two police cruisers, and the whole time, I'm seeing more cracks pop up in this story by the second. Why had I never questioned this? When I cut the engine, Kane's looking at me helplessly, his hands in his lap. "What?" I ask.

"I don't know what you're hoping to find. What can Officer Paradis actually tell us that we don't already know?"

"We're missing something. He might have some information from the scene."

Kane closes his eyes and inhales, long and purposefully. "Really? You're forgetting, Hail. I saw the scene," he says, his voice hollow. He had, for a second, until his father had pulled him back, but I'm sure that second is permanently ingrained in his head, as much as he won't speak of it. "You ever think how I might feel? Maybe I don't want to relive it."

With the car's heat off, the cold quickly seeps in. I dig my hands into the pockets of my coat, sinking into my seat. "Well, whose idea was it to torch the shed afterward? Isn't that odd? Do you—"

"My dad did that. It was easier that way. Easier than…going in there, I guess. He just wanted to wipe the place off the earth. And I agreed with him. We all did."

"But he did it so soon. Maybe he was hiding something that—"

"Wait, hold up." He turns to me in the passenger seat. I can feel his stare on me. "Do you realize what you're saying? You're implying that my dad had something to do with the death of his stepson. My. Dad. That's bullshit, Hailey. He loved Declan like a son."

"I know, I know." It's stupid. But my mind keeps spiraling, coming up with the weirdest ideas. Everything is on the table, and no one is safe from suspicion.

Not even Kane. Not even me.

53 Days Before

I was beyond jazzed.

School had let out for winter break, and I was lying in bed, savoring that invincible, one-whole-week-off feeling. I was making plans for the new year, wild ones. I'd learn French, because that was alluring, unlike Spanish, which my parents had been making me take because they insisted it would benefit me in the corporate world.

Maybe I'd apply for my first real summer job that didn't involve babysitting rich camp kids. I'd care more about my appearance: I'd use whatever money I got for Christmas and buy pieces for my wardrobe that I could accessorize with the help of YouTube so that everyone would think I was an artsy, classy chick. Maybe I'd dye my hair blue. I still didn't have a thing, but I was okay with it. Like Declan said, it was okay. *Not* having a thing was my thing.

And when Declan went off to UPenn (he hadn't gotten

accepted yet, but he was a shoo-in), I'd visit him in Philadelphia every weekend. He'd show me off to all the jealous girls in his dorm, and we'd walk down the city streets, hand in hand, like real adults. We'd stop in little shops and admire the offerings, and we'd share an ice cream cone. I could see him dropping to his knee and proposing, like he'd talked about. As ridiculous as it had sounded when he'd first mentioned it, I'd gradually warmed to the idea.

At this time, next year, I could be Mrs. Declan Weeks.

I grinned as the doorbell rang downstairs. I checked my phone. It was after noon. Throwing my hoodie over my PINK tank top, I scuffed into my giant unicorn slippers and ran downstairs. I opened the door to Declan. He was holding a tiny wrapped box.

He narrowed his eyes at me. "Let me guess. You just woke up."

I nodded. "Hell yes. It's the first day of winter break." I motioned to the box. "Is that for me?"

"It's actually for your mom," he said as I pushed open the screen door for him. "Of course it's for you, dummy."

I grinned. Then I read the little Christmas-tree-shaped card on the top, and my expression soured. "'Do not open until Xmas'... really? Why give it to me now? Scumbag."

He dug his hands into his pockets and looked sheepish. I knew him so well that I found myself bracing for the big bomb drop. "Because my stepdad surprised us with a trip to Split Rock Lodge," he said. "We leave this afternoon."

"What?"

He let out a bitter laugh. "You know me and winter sports," he said, twirling a pointer finger in the air. "Woo-hoo. I mean, why go to church on Christmas when you can freeze your ass off on top of a mountain?"

"But…our first Christmas together as a couple," I said, pouting. Not that I'd expected us to cavort through multicolored light displays while having a snowball fight and drinking hot cocoa as carolers regaled us, but, well…okay, I had been imagining something like that. Something romantic. Him being a hundred miles away kind of threw a wrench in that plan.

"I know, I know. Believe me, I'll be having a worse time than you will be," he said. "But I'll be back for New Year's."

I groaned. That was more than a week away. What the heck was I going to do?

The truth was, I shouldn't have complained. Earlier in the week, I'd reminded myself to count my blessings. Although Declan might have been destined to have a bad time and my week would be boring, I knew someone who'd be having an even worse time. Luisa's dad's heart attack had been pretty severe, and he'd lost a lot of oxygen to the brain, which had put him in a coma. He'd woken up three weeks later, permanently brain damaged, to the point that he couldn't communicate with his family.

Luisa and her family had always gone on extravagant vacations for the holidays, but this year, they'd canceled their Mediterranean cruise. I hadn't asked her what they were doing instead, because I hadn't wanted to pry, but every day, she'd come into school, her eyes red-rimmed from crying. She avoided her friends, and Kane said that she'd been avoiding him too.

"What will we do on New Year's?" I asked.

"I'd say it's an intimate get-together at our place. But you know Kane." He imitated an explosion with his hands. "He wants to do a speakeasy theme."

"Speakeasy? You mean, like, Roaring Twenties? *Gatsby*? He hated that book."

"Yeah, but the extravagance is right up his alley. And our parents will be out of town. You'll come, right?"

I nodded, wondering how I'd find a flapper dress. But there was no place I'd rather be.

My eyes drifted to the gift, carefully wrapped in red foil paper, in my hands. I gnawed on my lower lip. The box was the size of an engagement ring, but I didn't think Declan was that crazy to propose to me when I was sixteen. "I really have to wait until Christmas?"

"Hell no. I only did that to torture you," he said, grinning. "Annnd I see it worked. Open it."

Within seconds, I'd ripped off the paper. I lifted the lid to reveal a tiny silver heart. There was a diamond in the center. "Oh!"

"Do you like it?"

I nodded and took it out. The necklace was so delicate, but so, so pretty. I didn't really have that much fine jewelry. I handed it to him, whirled around, and lifted my hair so he could place it around my neck and fasten it.

"Diamonds are forever. And so are we," he'd whispered in my ear. As corny as it sounded, I liked it. *We're forever.* It made all those thoughts of walking the streets of Philadelphia next fall, hand in hand, and his bended-knee proposal, solidify in my mind. He kissed my ear. "I read that on a jewelry ad."

I shook my head at him as if he was a total nut and modeled the necklace, doing my best *Vogue* poses.

"Oh yeah. The unicorn slippers really pull the outfit together."

I kicked him in the shin with one pointy, stuffed horn, but it probably felt like being hit with a pillow.

"I'm gonna text you," he said to me. "Perpetually. From in front of the fire in the lodge. Where I'll be bored as hell. And having no fun whatsoever."

"I'm counting on it," I teased him.

It turned out he didn't text me much. The first couple of days he did, all the time. He texted about how the food sucked and snow sucked and everything about that particular area of the world sucked. By Christmas, he'd texted me twice, once to say, *Merry Christmas, love,* and another time, he texted a picture of him and Kane in front of a massive Christmas tree at the lodge.

After that, nothing. But I didn't mind.

Well, I minded a little. But I reminded myself that on New Year's Eve, we'd be together, and everything would be okay.

Wednesday, February 27

Of course, the little snow holiday we were having couldn't last forever.

At six thirty in the morning, the temperature is frigid. An icy wind is blowing off the retention pond. I rush out of the house, slide into my Jeep, slam the door, and power up the defrost. The windows are covered with icy starbursts, but I'll let Kane use the scraper. I sit there, teeth chattering, waiting for warmth to toast my frozen face.

Kane shows up late and slides in. He screams something that sounds like "Witch's tit! Mother of hell!" but I can't really tell because he's breathing into his hands at the same time.

Okay, forget Kane using the scraper. "You are such a wuss," I say to him, watching as he positions the vents so they're on him. He even tries to position one of *my* vents to blow on him, but I slap his hand away. "How is your mom? When are they coming home?"

"My dad was home last night. But Cooper the Pooper's in NICU. It'll be another few days until they bring him home."

"Oh. Is everything okay?" He's leaning over the heat, letting it blow straight into his face, not answering me. I smack him. "Oh my God, wuss. Grow a pair."

He gives me a superior glance. "All right, then this wuss won't tell you what he remembered about January 7 of last year."

"You remembered something?"

He nods.

Frozen windshield forgotten, I turn, scrabbling for my backpack. I reach in and pull out my little notebook, hovering my pen over the blank spot for that Sunday. "What?"

"Luisa's dad died."

I let out a hard breath of air. It's still so cold inside the Jeep that it puffs out as a white cloud between us. "Her dad is dead?"

He nods.

I didn't know that. Or maybe I did, once. I only knew her father from the few times he'd shown up at school concerts. Mostly, he worked. He was a workaholic. "From the heart attack?"

"So you can remember that, but not that he died?"

"Yeah, because that happened months before. In September, I think. She told her mother she was going to stay overnight with me because she didn't want to be alone. And then she went to stay with you."

"No. I was asleep. She tried to get in, but I was dead to the world. That goddamn *Gatsby* book drained me of my will to live."

"You never finished it?"

"I skimmed the good parts—all three pages of them—before the test. I think I passed." He stares through the defrosted circle that has appeared on the windshield. "She probably knocked on my door, but I didn't answer. So she must have gone back to your house."

I remembered her coming in my bedroom that night, so late that I didn't bother to check my phone to see what time it was. She had to come back anyway, because despite how many times they defied the rules, the Weeks boys weren't technically allowed to have girls in their rooms overnight. "I was dead to the world by then too."

"Yeah. Fucking *Gatsby*."

I don't bother to tell him that I actually liked the book, once I read it. I liked Jay, the way he was so dedicated to Daisy and zealous about pursuing his dream of being with her. Tragic, yes, but I guess I understood him. I understood how reality was often tainted and never could match up with the dream.

I write down the new information about Luisa's father dying. "Do you remember anything else?"

"Just that it really messed with her. She came to my house that night, talking crazy. She was saying shit about you, unbelievable stuff. I don't remember. We all wanted to go to her dad's funeral, which was a couple days after that, but by then she wouldn't even talk to me. She told me she didn't want any of us there."

"Well, she was sad."

"It was more than that. She was pissed on New Year's, and then after you guys got into that fight at the movies…she didn't want anything to do with any of us. She said her mother might move them away to live with family in Massachusetts, and she wanted to go. To be rid of us all."

"But…why?"

He shrugs.

Luisa's family never moved. They stayed, and eventually, somehow, she and Kane had patched things up, rising to become the untouchable power couple of our senior class. "You guys got back together."

"Not for a long time," he says. "We only started going out again in September. She didn't want anything to do with me for months."

"Why?"

He rolls his eyes. "Because she's Luisa. She needed her"—he makes quotation signs at his ears—"space."

I pull out of the driveway, heading for school, deep in my own head. Kane always thinks every relationship woe he's ever had with Luisa boils down to her wild, unexplained mood swings, but I don't believe it. There's got to be more to their fights than that.

"I'm breaking up with her, though. Today," he says.

Keeping my eyes on the road ahead, I see him in the periphery of my vision, studying me, waiting for my reaction. I don't have one.

"You have anything to say about that?" he prompts.

"Nope." I told him that's the last thing I want. He thinks I'm so interested in having a boyfriend. After the way everything turned out with the last one? I don't look at him, but I can tell from the way he clenches his fists in his lap that he's pissed.

We don't say anything more due to the roar of the wind outside.

By the time we arrive at the senior parking lot, I know what I need to do. "Don't break up with her yet, okay?" I say to him as I find one of the last open spaces. "Please?"

He was trying to zip his coat higher to his chin, but he stops, staring at me. "Why?"

"Just don't. Okay?"

I don't tell him what I'm planning, because I know he'll try to talk me out of it. But I need to talk to Luisa. She already hates me. I don't need to give her another reason to.

45 Days Before

The party was raging before ten. Mr. and Mrs. Weeks were gone, and my parents had gone to New York to see the ball drop, so all of Fox Court was choked with teen cars. They parked on the lawns, in the woods, backed up against one another like in a used car lot. Music pumped and light blared from every window.

"This is more of a speak*hard*, do you not think?" Javier asked me. It was clear Javier came from a culture way more sophisticated than ours, because he never drank to excess. He'd told us the drinking age in Spain was sixteen, but Europeans are way more casual about drinking in general and rarely got shitfaced. So he usually absorbed all our naïve American antics with amusement and was our responsible designated driver. He picked a half-deflated Santa lawn decoration off the floor. "Where did this come from?"

I had no clue. The party was about three minutes from

dissolving into total chaos. Most people hadn't gotten the speak-easy memo, so only ten people were dressed up. I had on one of my mom's dresses. Even though it was modern, it had fringe on the hem, but I felt ridiculously stupid and old lady, so I'd changed into jeans. Luisa was wearing the full flapper outfit, complete with headband and minidress, and looked like she could've come out of the twenties. Kane was wearing a suit, but he was the only one, because most guys had no clue how to dress. It was a flop, as far as themes went, but as far as parties went, it was shaping up to be the most talked-about event of the new year.

"You know what?" Nina said to me, unable to keep her eyes open as she lay on the living room couch. She was badly balancing one of Mrs. Weeks's martini glasses in her hand, but there wasn't a martini in there. The liquid was purplish, and it smelled noxious. Her sparkly fringed dress, the one I'd thought looked so chic when she'd come in at nine, just looked rumpled and sad, and her dark bob was falling in her face. Her eyeliner was smeared, and her face was shiny. "I love you. I really do."

"I know, dear," I said as she closed her eyes and her head lolled onto my shoulder. I patted her arm and took a swig of my beer as her head lolled back to her boyfriend's shoulder.

She looked up at him, as if seeing him for the first time. "And I love you too! Really, really, I do. I want to make babies with you."

I groaned and loosened her death grip from my shoulder, then slid out of the way. "I think I will leave you to it, then." I winked at Javier. "Just maybe not right here, or right now."

In the time that Mrs. Weeks had moved in, she'd gradually added the needed woman's touch. The furniture was nice, there was actual art on the walls, and the carburetor had been moved off the center island. So what was happening was a shame. There were bottles on every surface, bodies crammed into every space, and knickknacks were being broken or ruined at an alarming pace. I reached over to steady Nina's drink before the white couch became the next victim.

Luisa was at the kitchen table, sitting on Kane's lap as they played Quarters, the little feather in her headband bobbing and fists pumping as she celebrated landing a shot. Everyone seemed pretty smashed, or getting there, because Kane, wonder that he was, had only secured alcohol from one of his old teammates, and *not a lick of food*. There were some pizzas in the freezer that disappeared earlier—though I wasn't sure anyone had actually cooked them, because I never saw the oven on—and a wilted, half-eaten salad container from Wendy's that Mrs. Weeks had left over disappeared too. It was all very bizarre. These people were like locusts. I hadn't seen Declan in an hour and hoped he hadn't succumbed to the swarm.

I went upstairs to check, navigating bodies and garbage on the stairs. The door to his room was locked. I banged on it and called his name, but no one answered.

So I went outside and climbed the trellis. I'd gotten to be a pro at it. I peeked in his window. He was wearing headphones and lying on his bed, face up, a tented magazine across his middle. I waved and knocked until he noticed me. He ripped off his headphones, pushed open the window, and dove back onto his bed. "Hey, stranger."

"Oh my God, Declan," I said, climbing inside and flopping onto the bed beside him. The beat of the bass downstairs made the mattress vibrate pleasantly. I was already buzzed, but I'd left my beer downstairs, so it wouldn't last long unless I went back down. "You have to see what's going on down there. Everyone's letting loose."

He picked up his magazine. "Nah. Not my thing. Thus, the locked door."

Being with Declan for the past year, I'd made partying not *my* thing too. But what was going on downstairs? It was a train wreck. I knew people would be talking about it in school, and I didn't want to miss the gory details. "Yeah, but…don't you want to dance?"

His mouth turned down in distaste. *So, that's a no.*

"Darn it," I said to him. "I should have gotten film for my new camera. I could've taken pictures of us, but I only have one left."

"Where's your phone?"

"Charging. The battery life is terrible. I think I need a new one."

"Too bad."

I rolled over and looked at him. I'd never actually seen Declan in a mood. But this was one.

"Is everything okay?"

"I'm just thinking about how I'm going to have to clean up this hole tomorrow," he said. "You know Kane will sleep until dinnertime."

"It's not a big deal. I can help."

When he set down his *Rolling Stone*, I knew that that wasn't all of it. "Also. I've been thinking. About the future."

I should've known. Declan was always thinking heavy thoughts. I wished he could relax and not think about heavy things for just one night. Have fun. Hell, especially on New Year's Eve. "You have to think about that stuff tonight?"

"It's a new year, Hail. You ever wonder where you'll be next year at this time? What you'll have accomplished? Whether you'll be better off, or worse?"

I smiled, and those thoughts I'd had earlier in the winter vacation flooded me again. "You'll have graduated high school. And you'll be at Penn. And we'll be together, Declan. Right?"

He nodded.

Set in stone, I'd thought. *We're forever.* "So what's there to worry about?"

He put up a finger. "I never said I was worrying. Just thinking."

I sighed. "Anyone ever tell you that you think too much?"

"Yes. You."

I checked the clock on his nightstand. It was still an hour until midnight. "Don't you want to kiss me at midnight?"

His face broke out in a grin. "Why wait 'til midnight? Come here."

I tilted my chin toward him, and he leaned down and gave me a very chaste kiss, then started to put his arm around me. I knew where we were headed. Hours and hours of fooling around. Declan was still frustrating me, since I always knew where we would stop. I wriggled out of his arms and stood up.

"You know what? I think I'll go down for a little longer. But I'll be back up for midnight. Or…you can come down?"

He frowned and shook his head slowly.

"Fine," I grumbled, giving him the finger. He grabbed my extended middle finger with his own and we had a little sword fight with them. I laughed, but that was more the beer than anything else. Deep down, I was disappointed. And maybe he was disappointed with me too.

Downstairs, I breathed in the chaos excitedly. Kane was now at the center island, doling out orange Jell-O shots. He had on an Abraham Lincoln hat, no clue where that'd come from, and again I wished my phone was working, or I had more than one stinking shot left in my camera. I took a Jell-O shot and let the orange glob tumble down my throat, squeezing the paper cup to get the whole thing out. "Where's Luisa?" I asked him.

"Lying down somewhere," he said. "She wasn't feeling well."

"Oh." I plucked another shot off the tray, and one for good luck, since they were going fast. I knocked the next one against his, and we downed them at the same time. "Cheers. Happy New Year."

The third wasn't as neat; some dribbled off my chin. That was a perfect portent for the direction the rest of the evening would head. Things just got sloppier and sloppier. By midnight, I was huddled over a toilet, puking my guts out. I'd wanted to be present for the whole party, but I missed everything after that third shot. I recalled flashes, blurs, people coming and going, screaming, scraping my elbow, sloppy kisses, laughing until it hurt, crying until I couldn't breathe. But in the morning, I couldn't recall the why behind any of it.

When I woke in that new year, mouth sour, head pounding, I didn't even know how I'd made it to my own bed.

Wednesday, February 27

Actually speaking to Luisa ends up being more difficult than I thought. I text her as soon as I get to gym class: **Can we talk?**

Right away, the message shows itself as being read, so I know she got it. But after two periods, she still hasn't responded. Which means she's avoiding me.

Since Luisa and Kane stopped hanging out with us at my locker in the morning, I have no idea about her schedule or where to find her. I'm in the advanced classes, but she's on the honors track, so we don't share a single period. Whenever I see her, she's with Kane. I manage to ask around and find out that she's in third period study hall, so instead of making my way to class, I head to the cafeteria.

I poke my head in, but she's not there. When I'm about to give up, I see her making her way past the award showcases toward me. When she sees me, her eyes narrow slightly. She approaches, looking up and down the hallway as if she's afraid to be seen with me, and says, "The answer's no. I don't want to talk to you."

"Come on, Luisa. I—"

"No," she says. "Kane told me what you're up to. And I don't really care what happened to you when you were in the hospital. I'm not going to feel sorry for you."

I've never actually heard Luisa, usually all sunshine and sweetness, sound so cold.

Or maybe I have. Something about this exchange feels familiar. *We've fought before.*

She crosses her arms, hugging her notebook to her chest. I'm not sure if it's possible for her to hate me any more than she does in this moment. Her tone could only be about one thing. Kane. Kane giving me a flower on Valentine's Day. Kane hanging with me at the party, when he should have been with her. "I know you hate me. But I want to know what happened the days before Declan died."

She laughs bitterly. "What happened? Kane said your mind was messed up. You really don't remember anything?"

I shake my head. "I really don't."

"That's probably a good thing. Because if I did what you'd done, I don't think I could show myself in public again," she says.

My skin blooms with goose bumps. "What do you mean?"

"You used to look at me like I was pathetic, because I loved

Kane, even though he wasn't the best of boyfriends. But you know what?" Her pretty face is wrapped in a snarl. "You were worse. In fact, you're so obsessed with the Weeks boys that you didn't want anyone else to have them."

I stand there, frozen. People sweep by us in the hallway, but some drag their feet, watching as Luisa rails at me, her voice gradually getting louder.

Luisa getting riled up is enough to gain attention, but when she starts poking me in the chest with every word, more people stop. I back away, until I'm pressed against the wall. "So if you don't remember what happened, I'll fill you in. The last time I spoke to you was at Declan's funeral. I told you that you and I were done as friends, and that I didn't want to see your face again. And I mean it. You disgusted me then, and even more now."

My face is hot. People around us are whispering. Tears threaten to pour from my eyes. "But why?"

"Why do you think?" She looks around, surprised by the crowd that's gathered. She leans in and whispers, "He told me how you hounded him. All those games you played. If you want to know who's responsible for Declan's death, look in the mirror."

She spins on her heel, opening the door to the cafeteria and sliding inside, as the period bell clangs above me.

39 Days Before

The first week back to school after winter break sucked.
The high temperatures were in the single digits, and all the
Christmas presents and decorations and cheer that made winter
fun were over. Summer wasn't in sight. All we had on our schedules? Months of more bleak, dark cold. The only thing I could
say I was looking forward to? Valentine's Day. Ordinarily, I
dreaded the holiday, but this was my first Valentine's Day as part
of a couple.

I. Couldn't. Wait.

About a year ago, if you asked me, I would've rolled my eyes
and said Valentine's Day was commercialism at its finest. But
now? I'd pictured it: those goofy flowers the Key Club was offering for purchase? I was all over that. Didn't matter that the actual
day was more than a month away; I'd already gotten the form and
written out my message to him.

D—I love you, you amazing, wonderful, gorgeous but also completely insane person, you.—H

Maybe I'd buy Declan an enormous chocolate heart too—if I had the time and funds.

I also thought I could put together a book of our selfies. He had taken a thousand of them of us together, always texting the best ones to me, and now that I had a new camera, I knew there'd be more. I'd have to go to the craft store to get a nice scrapbook, but he'd appreciate it. Declan was sentimental that way, which was why he kept mementos of our life together— movie tickets, napkins from restaurants we visited, things like that.

I was visibly cheerier than everyone else in our group. The ones who showed up to school all went around like zombies, still getting over their New Year's hangovers. But Kane, Declan, and Luisa all had a stomach flu that kept each of them out for much of the week. And our pre-first-period meetings had stopped includ-ing all six of us. So I decided to rally the troops. We should all do something over the weekend.

I set up a group message: **Movies. This weekend. YOU MUST BE IN.**

Kane responded first: K.

He was notoriously terse when it came to texting.

Then Nina, who had to know everything: **What are we going to see?**

Javier responded with: **You get to spend 2 hours in the dark with me**

Declan was last: **What time?**

Luisa never responded, but I heard from Kane that she was up for it. We arranged to meet at eight at the Grand, which is this old-style one-screen movie house on Main Street. Since I arranged it, I told the boys I'd drive them and we'd pick up Luisa on the way, but Kane bailed on me and told me Luisa would pick him up, so it was only me and Declan.

When Declan showed up at my door, I waved the paper for my Key Club carnation in front of his face. "Guess what this is?"

His eyes followed it. "Paper?"

"Funny. No, it's my secret message for you. But you won't find out what it says until Valentine's Day." I folded it and wiggled my eyebrows cryptically. "Intrigued?"

"Very." He nodded slowly. "Actually, I have no idea what you're talking about."

I stuffed the paper into my purse. "You know. The Key Club does that flower fund-raiser every February fourteenth. I've never had an occasion to buy one before."

"Oh. Right. I have the paper at home. When are they due?"

"By the thirty-first. So you have time to think of eloquent, inspired words of passion. If, by chance, there was someone you wanted to send one to," I said, giving him an innocent look.

He tapped his chin. "I'll have to think on that one."

"Snot." I jumped into his arms and kissed him. "I feel like I haven't seen you in forever."

"That's the first kiss you've given me this year, you know," he said. His eyes didn't sparkle the way they usually did, and he kept his hands in his pockets as I kissed him. Cool, aloof, his body tense, like a rod. Something was wrong.

It hit me that I was supposed to have gone back up to his room that night. Hadn't I? I guess I hadn't. He'd gotten a stomach bug right after that, so I thought that was what was keeping us apart. I hadn't realized it was something else. "You're angry about New Year's."

He shook his head slightly. "Just tired."

I studied his face carefully. I would have apologized, had I known what I was apologizing for. But the rest of New Year's Eve after I'd done Jell-O shots was still a blur. Nina and Javier had gone on and on about some hilarious antics, but I'd missed most of that. I hadn't been the subject of any of those good gossip-worthy stories, but that didn't mean I hadn't done anything gossip-worthy. Maybe it meant that no one had the guts to remind me of what I'd done. That scared me.

We got into the car. I shoved the key in the ignition and

pumped the heat to ward off the frigid temperatures. Our favorite song came on the radio. Usually Declan usually would have remarked about it or sung along. Instead, he was silent.

I couldn't take it for another second. I said, "Tell me. Please. I can't take the silent treatment."

I was waving my hands, and he plucked the nearest one out of the air and held it between his two warm ones. He said, "You'd been drinking."

"But that's no excuse." I closed my eyes, hating myself. So I *had* done something horrible. "I'm sorry if I hurt you. What happened, Declan. Please."

He shrugged. "You were hanging all over my stepbrother."

I waited for him to say more, but he didn't.

"Is that all?" I laughed. "You know how Kane and I are. We always do things like that. He's like my brother."

He nodded, contemplating this, and I thought, *Okay, all is good.* Then he said, "This may be out of left field, because I've never had a sister, but I'm pretty sure that if I did, I wouldn't kiss her like that."

I froze, my hand in his, and despite the drafty Jeep, I felt my face heat. I had a sudden flash of memory of me in the Weeks living room, bombed, kissing a number of people. I recalled kissing Kane, but what I'd thought felt so right—the warm, soft pleasant feeling of his tongue melding with mine—now hit me like a wall of bricks. How incredibly wrong it was. How incredibly wrong *I* was.

And I'd wanted Declan to send me a flower? I was lucky he was still speaking to me.

"God," I breathed. "I didn't... I mean, I didn't know..."

There was no explanation for it. Saying I was smashed didn't seem to be enough, because it still made me a jerk, since I'd gone and gotten myself that way. He shrugged, reached out, and smoothed my hair behind my shoulder. "It's okay, Hail. It's okay."

"Don't be so nice about it!" I said to him. "Yell at me. That was horrible. Oh my God."

Suddenly, going out to the movies seemed like an exceedingly stupid idea. I wanted to crawl in a hole and die. At that moment, I vowed never to drink again.

Instead, I said, "Declan. I love you. I don't think of Kane that way *at all*. I must have been out of my mind. I am so sorry."

He nodded. "I know you are. It's already forgotten."

But I could tell that it was still on his mind. Maybe I knew him too well. Declan felt emotions deeply, and I knew there were some scars in his life that he'd never forget, that he'd take to the grave. This would be one of them. This was my first relationship, so I didn't realize it then, but sometimes the most innocent mistake can cause two people to stop heading in one direction and begin moving in another direction entirely. I felt like we'd turned that corner, and I didn't like where we were going.

And God, I would've given anything to turn us back.

But I couldn't cancel my little get-together. I'd orchestrated it. So I drove him to the theater, and we barely talked at all. I tried to convince myself it was because the wind ripping through the top made it too hard to carry on a conversation, but that had never stopped us before.

The small, old theater was more crowded than I'd ever seen it. There was only street parking, and I had to parallel park, which I hate, in a spot about six blocks from Main. When we finally got to the lobby of the theater, it was after eight, and the movie had already started.

Nina, Javier, Luisa, and Kane were standing outside, waiting for us. When Luisa whirled to look at me, I stopped in my tracks.

Her stare fell on me, cold, and she didn't say a word. No doubt she knew about what had happened on New Year's Eve. Maybe she'd even seen us.

Oh God. Could this be any more of a nightmare? No wonder she hadn't responded to my text about the movies. She hated me.

I avoided eye contact with her as we approached. Kane said, "Should we bother? We won't get seats together."

We all agreed to go in anyway, because it was a horror movie that all of us wanted to see, and the previews usually took fifteen minutes anyway. It would have been a blessing that I didn't have to sit next to Kane or Luisa anyhow. But when we got in the theater, there was only one grouping of three, one grouping of two, and single seats everywhere else.

Luisa climbed into the grouping of three, then looked at me defiantly, as if laying down a challenge. I wasn't going there and wasn't going to split up Nina and Javier, so I ended up sitting by myself in the back corner of the theater.

The movie was terrible. I watched the heads of Luisa, Kane, and Declan, silhouetted in the light from the movie screen, feeling like shit. Luisa was sitting between them, in the spot meant for me. Somehow she had gotten the two Weeks boys, and I got the back row next to an elderly lady who smelled like old cheese and kept elbowing me in an epic battle over the armrest.

When I saw Luisa stand to leave midmovie, I pushed out of the seat and went after her, intent on clearing the air.

"Luisa," I called before she could go into the ladies' room.

She turned. "Don't. Don't even. You've always wanted Kane, and then I find out you actually slept with him?"

I stared at her in shock. How had she found out? I hadn't told anyone, so the answer was obvious. Kane.

"N-no," I stammered in a hoarse whisper, looking back at the darkened movie theater. The last thing I needed was for Declan to follow us out and hear this. "That was a long time ago. And we were stupid. And it didn't—"

"It didn't mean anything, and yet you couldn't keep your hands off him on New Year's?"

"I was—"

"Drunk. Don't give me that excuse. I see the way you look at him. You've always hated him being with anyone else, because you never wanted anyone else to have him. Admit it."

My face grew hot. "No, I—"

Her gaze trailed past me. I looked over my shoulder. Kane stood behind us. Had he heard that? Shaking my head, I dodged Kane's worried looks and stalked back into the theater, where I could disguise my tears.

I cried quietly to myself through the rest of the movie, until the end credits rolled.

Thursday, February 28

Kane bailed on a ride home, and a ride into school the next day, so I now have this irrational feeling he's avoiding me. Maybe it's because of my talk with Luisa.

If you want to know who killed Declan, look in the mirror. She's insane, of course. Jealous, because I had Declan *and* Kane.

Or at least I thought I did.

The next time I see Kane, it's in the science hallway. He has his tongue down Luisa's throat, which only makes me feel more alone. Guess the whole "breakup" isn't really happening.

All yesterday and this morning, I've been replaying Luisa's words in my head. She said that I hounded Declan. She thinks I failed him. That I'm responsible for his death. And I don't even know what I did.

I have to know. Even if Kane thinks I won't like what I find out. It can't be worse than not knowing.

When I get back home after school, I can't bother with my trig homework. I reach under my bed and pull out the box of stuff from Declan's room. Since my parents are at work, I bring it downstairs, setting it on the coffee table, then open the flaps. This time, I dig through the entire box, pulling out ticket stubs from movies and concerts we'd gone to, napkins, matchbooks, toothpicks, all the junk that signified our life together. He'd piled them all in the top drawer of the dresser in his bedroom. I find the one for that cheesy horror movie. The last movie we'd seen in the theaters, and he hadn't even really been with me. He'd sat next to Luisa and Kane, while I'd sat alone.

Then I notice a stub for another movie. It's a romantic comedy, a movie I know I've never seen. My eyes scan the date. January 16 of last year. A midnight showing, one month before his death.

I stare at it. Declan liked romantic movies about as much as the next guy. Basically, he stomached them for me. But he'd gone to this movie…alone?

Declan often liked to be alone with his thoughts. Still, I couldn't imagine him spending much contemplative time at a midnight showing of a Reese Witherspoon flick.

I check my phone. January 16 had been a Tuesday. Declan was usually one to cut things short on school nights so he could prepare for school and get a good night's sleep for the next day.

Nothing short of an emergency would've drawn him out of the house that late.

Unless...

My skin prickles. He went with someone else. To be alone with someone else.

I drop the stub into the box as if it's a hot flame, and text Kane: **Do you think Declan was seeing someone else?**

No response. No three dancing dots. I stare at the phone, willing him to answer, then dig through the box again. I find a little stuffed bear but can't figure out why Declan would have it. Did he have a history with someone else? Did he have mementos of a whole other life I knew nothing about? I feel sick, dizzy. Suddenly, everything inside that box is suspicious, even the most innocuous items, like the Holy Bible. *Do you not know that the unrighteous will not inherit the kingdom of God?*

Oh God.

My phone buzzes with a message from Kane. I jump on it and read: **Why?**

I'm going to be sick. The room swims as I type. **A movie ticket I found in the box his mom gave me.**

I want him to say that I'm being ridiculous and paranoid, that Declan was too good to do such a thing. Instead, his next message is: **Can I come over?**

No. I sink down onto the couch and gather a blanket around

me, hoping to ward off the chill that's suddenly sunk into my bones. Because there is only one reason Kane would delay answering me. **Why? Just tell me.**

I don't think you'll like the answer.

I draw in a breath, my body trembling. It's nearly impossible to get my fingers to spell out my next text, because I'm half-blind from the tears in my eyes: **So he was.**

I think so.

Who? But I already know the answer. Maybe I'd known it all along. **Luisa, right?**

Yeah.

Turns out, I was wrong. There is something worse than not knowing. And it's knowing.

I'm not sure what happens after that. All I know is that I crash, my body collapsing in on itself, and every ounce of will that I'd been able to muster since I got out of Shady Harbor evaporates. All that's left is pain. It's so bad that I feel like I might die from it. Time speeds up and slows down at the same time, stretching and spiraling thoughts through my head. Declan, kissing me in the playhouse. Declan, the first time I met him, playing that guitar. Declan, singing that song to me on my sixteenth birthday. Declan, dead, his brains splayed out on the plywood wall of the shed. My world is ending. I wonder if this is how he felt before he ended his.

Before I know it, Kane is sitting on the edge of the couch, holding a tissue box, watching me. My face is covered in tears and snot, and I know there's plenty more where that came from. My parents usually don't get home until seven on weekdays, and despite the darkness, it's probably not yet dinnertime. He holds out a tissue, but I don't have the energy to take it.

"When?" My voice is choked.

"I don't know when it started. I think after New Year's, last year. But maybe it was before then, and we just never noticed."

After New Year's. After they saw Kane and me kissing. Was it revenge? Was that all it was? Declan didn't strike me as someone to be vindictive. And I'd apologized, he'd accepted. It didn't make sense. "Why?"

"I don't..." He stops. "I have something to tell you," he says.

Curled in a ball, I don't say a word. I don't like the tone of his voice. I don't really want to know any more. It's too much. My heart aches. Maybe it actually is broken. It feels heavy, swollen, on the verge of bursting.

"I told you Luisa suspected something was going on between us," he says. "But she didn't suspect. She knew. Because I told her."

I don't say anything. I was right. I can't hurt worse. I only feel numb. "But nothing was going on between us."

"Something was," he goes on. "I guess you and I... We kissed at midnight. And it was more than a little kiss. It got out of hand,

Hailey. Luisa started asking me question after question about whether I wanted you or thought of you in that way, and I…" He shakes his head. "I was sick of it. So I told her. I told her what we'd done when we were fifteen."

It's so ludicrous that neither of us can say it. Like it was so much of a mistake that we can't admit that we had sex. I roll over on the couch, facing him. "And she told Declan."

He nods.

"He hated me. He hated me after that. Everything I'd ever told him was a lie. And he…" I suck in a breath. All that time, he'd known. It would have been bad enough if he'd confronted me, but he never did…which was worse. He'd let the knowledge fester, stopped going to church, started seeing Luisa, and then…

"Hailey. I'm sorry. But Declan wasn't unbalanced. He didn't kill himself because of that."

"He didn't kill himself at all!" I fire back. I'm surer of that than I've ever been. Still, I know that sex was huge to him. All he ever did was talk about our first time. *Our* first time. And I never told him. I never admitted that everything he thought he knew about me was a lie.

I let out a choked sob.

"Hey," Kane says, sitting me up and putting an arm around me. "Come on."

"I'm the worst person ever," I sob, my body racked with

convulsions. "I lied to him through our whole relationship. He had every right to get back at me."

"And then you got back at him," Kane says quietly.

"What?"

He reaches into his backpack and pulls out a small bag. From it, he pulls a strawberry-colored Fujifilm Instax camera. I stare at it, two and two coming together in my mind. I remember sitting in front of the Christmas tree, unwrapping this gift as my parents snapped pictures, pretending I was six years old, and me indulging them since it was the first time since I'd gotten my car that they weren't at each other's throats. I'd kissed them both, then, since Declan wasn't around, taken a bunch of pictures of the snowy outside before realizing I should have saved the film for New Year's.

THIS ENDS HERE.

"This is your camera," he says. "You took that picture of them. You showed it to me. You're the one who gave that picture to Declan."

26 Days Before

"You're coming with me," Nina said, grabbing my hand and yanking me toward the stairwell.

It was Friday afternoon, and I was congratulating myself on having survived what had been the worst two weeks of school ever. Not only did I have to deal with Luisa's eye daggers, but Kane and I had agreed to maintain a distance, because we didn't want to cast any more suspicion on ourselves. I knew that was a good move, but it didn't stop me from missing him.

But I missed Declan more. We went on as if life was the same, but there was a subtle shift. Every time Declan blew me off, despite having a good excuse, I worried. In the first weeks of the new year, he was always busy with some school project. This time was worse than when he'd ignored me before. He wasn't fixing up a new car for me. He said he was busy because he'd missed classes while he was out with the flu, but he definitely didn't have the senioritis that had hit most Deer Hills seniors.

It was more than that, though. Whenever we kissed, he felt stiff in my arms. I couldn't help but think he was imagining me kissing Kane. He'd never been much of a talker, but he was quieter than usual. I'd vowed to be extra sweet to him, bringing him an extra boat of french fries for lunch, leaving notes in his locker. He used to call me the best girlfriend ever and pull me into his arms every chance he got. Now he smiled mirthlessly, and we barely touched.

Our whole group of six had fractured, and it was all my fault.

"Where are we going?" I asked Nina, confused. It was after last period, and I'd gathered my books for weekend homework so I could make a quick getaway to the junior parking lot.

She winked at me and showed me three of her dad's credit cards. "To the mall. My dad was feeling generous last night."

"I thought we were going to the basketball game."

The Deer Hills High basketball team had finally gotten into the playoffs, which had never happened before, so the entire student body was having an unusual fit of school spirit. Deer Hills excelled at baseball and football, because of Kane. But we'd sucked at basketball. So everyone was wearing Deer Hills red today, and we'd had a big pep rally after lunch.

I'd noticed the problem then, when I'd seen Nina sitting alone, cheeks red, face scrunched in a snarl. Nina never sat alone. Javier was so attached to her that he might as well have been a wart.

She shook her head. "Not us. You really care about basketball?"

The answer to that was no. But I did care that the six of us would finally be together again. Maybe we could heal some rifts, bonding over our shared school spirit. Mostly, I wanted to heal with Declan. I wanted to make things right, so much so that if I could've subtracted years from my life in order to turn back time to before New Year's, I would have. "Well..."

"Javier and I broke up," Nina announced grandly.

"You did? Why?"

It wasn't much of a shock. They'd broken up at least three times that previous year, because they were polar opposites. "Because he's a turd, that's why. He's always looking at other girls. And then I heard he was flirting with a freshman saxophone player in band."

"Okay, but—"

"Luisa's not going, and—"

"She's not?"

"Yeah, have you noticed? She has the biggest stick up her butt, lately. Ever since New Year's. She doesn't want anything to do with us anymore."

Not us, I thought. *Me.*

"And I'm not going either, if it means being with Jav. So do

you really want to go to the ball game with the three stooges?"
she asked me. Without waiting for an answer, she said, "Thought
not! So you're coming with me. To the mall. I want to get a hot
outfit so I can show Javier what he can't have."

"Um…" I'd long since lost interest in the mall. Ever since
Declan and I had become a couple, I'd kind of let my appearance go, wearing jeans and sweatshirts everywhere, since I'd
been so comfortable with us. But maybe that hadn't been wise.
Maybe I should have been making more of an effort to look
nice for him. Despite having been in relationships for longer
than I'd been, Nina and Luisa always dressed to impress. I
could also get the stuff I needed for Declan's scrapbook project
at the mall…

Still, I didn't want to give up my chance to be with Declan.
That was what mattered. "I really should be with Declan. I haven't
had a chance to see him much."

She wrinkled her nose. "Really?"

"I'm sorry, but yeah," I said surely.

She huffed, then started to pout. "I can't believe you're going
to leave me alone in my time of need. I thought it was holes
before poles forever, girl."

"I'm sorry."

I was sorry, especially when I got to my car and saw Declan
leaning against it. "Hey," he said as I approached.

I leaned over to give him a kiss, a chaste one on his cheek that he didn't return. "You get the note I left in your locker?"

He nodded. "I did. Thanks."

It had been kind of corny, about how I was looking forward to going out with him that night. I wanted him to know that I thought of him, and only him. I wanted him to understand that I didn't care about Kane in the least. "Oh. So...you need a ride home?"

He shook his head. "I wanted to let you know I can't be there tonight. I've got a project to do for physics, and I'm just not feeling basketball. You know me and sports."

"Oh," I said, my spirits plummeting. *He's just not feeling it.* But I'd be there. Meaning he wasn't feeling *me.* "So what? You're going to sit at home alone, on a Friday?"

He cocked a grin my way. "Never stopped me before." He took my hand. "I'll make it up to you. Okay?"

I widened my eyes hopefully. "How?"

He let out a snort of a laugh. "I don't know. I'll think of something." Not having a romantic retort was so, so unlike Declan. "Have fun at the game. Text me who wins."

The idea of going to a game with Kane and Javier made me feel sick. I couldn't go with Kane. Didn't Declan know how awkward that'd be? Didn't Declan see how hard I'd been trying to avoid him? Or didn't he care? I started to tell him that I wasn't sure if I'd even go, but he checked the screen of his phone and cut me off.

"All right. I've got to go." He said it as if what I did made no difference to him, but he held my gloved hand in his and said, "Be safe."

At least he wants me to be safe. See? He does care. I stood on my tiptoes and kissed him, but as he leaned back against the hood of my Jeep, I had the oddest feeling that I was cornering him, that he was kissing me because he couldn't escape otherwise. He slid his arms around my waist, and I savored the feeling. That innocent touch was a lifeline. I kissed him longer than I should have, even after he tried to let go.

You hate me, I thought when I looked into his eyes. *Just tell me you do.*

But there was nothing in those eyes that told me anything. They used to speak the world to me. And they'd gone utterly dead. Declan didn't spew hate. Didn't even show it. He kept that inside. Always had.

The trip to the mall with Nina was the shopping trip from hell. I should've known. Nina was fashion-forward, and shopping was a marathon sport for her. We stayed at the mall until eight thirty, until my feet were aching and I wanted to cry. All I had to show for our excursion was an American Eagle sweater that I'd gotten on clearance. When Nina dropped me off at nine, the street was quiet. It was still early, as far as Fridays went. My parents were out, and it was likely the basketball game wouldn't be over for another couple of hours. I went inside and got myself a Coke, then texted Declan. **Home. Want me to come over?**

I waited for a response, but there was nothing. Sighing, I went upstairs and looked across Fox Court to his room.

There was only one light on in the entire Weeks house, his. Kane wouldn't be back for a while. So he was in there. Why wasn't he checking his phone?

I watched for a little longer, willing my phone to buzz, but it didn't.

I'd finally made the decision to go over when I saw a silhouette in the window. Just a shape, beyond the blinds.

And then another. They joined together, and my heart dropped.

I'm not sure what I was thinking when I did what I did next. I grabbed my camera, then hurried downstairs and out the door. I ran across the street to Declan's house, climbed the trellis and peeked inside.

At first, I saw nothing, and hoped what I'd seen was all a big misunderstanding. Maybe Kane had come home early. But when I moved to the side to see between the windowsill and the closed blinds, I saw the curved slope of Luisa's naked back, her white-blond hair tumbling down over her shoulders.

This was a mistake, I told myself, scrabbling forward on the roofing tiles, pushing ever closer to see something that would explain away what was happening inside.

Instead, the vision only got clearer. Luisa was naked, straddling him. Straddling my Declan. He had his hands around her backside, holding her on him. His top half was propped against the headboard, and he had a look on his face... It was the same look he'd given me outside the school that afternoon. Just... dead. He wasn't happy anymore. He held her as she moved on him, wriggling, bouncing, tossing her head back. I could hear her animal noises through the closed window. But he was so, so silent.

Revenge. That was the first thought that hit me. His. Mine. I felt the weight of the camera in my hand. I don't know why I'd been saving that last picture for our selfie. I'd take this picture and photocopy it, plaster it around school. Make them pay.

I raised the camera to the window, my eyes bleary with tears, unfocused. I snapped the picture, not caring what was in the screen as I watched him lurch forward, his hands tightening around her back as he came.

This was the boy who'd wanted to wait for marriage.

I went back to my house quietly and riffled through my jewelry box. I pulled out the tiny heart with the diamond and stared at it. Then I went in front of the mirror and put it on, trying to erase the images I'd just seen. Only two words stuck in my head as I climbed into bed, my eyes swollen from crying.

We're forever.

Friday, March 1

I roll over in bed and am hit by bright sunlight slashing through the blinds.

I'd barely slept all night. I'd turned the memory of Declan and Luisa over and over in my head. I tossed and turned, batting that new memory, letting it grow clearer, all the details solidifying in cinematic clarity.

Luisa had blamed me for Declan's death, not as his friend. She blamed me because she'd been in love with him. Declan was the easiest person to fall in love with. He had such a caring heart. If I hadn't known them so well, I might have thought they'd slept together to get revenge on Kane and me. But Luisa and Declan weren't as cold as Kane and I were. They'd cared about each other.

And that was what nearly killed me.

That look in his eyes that I wanted to believe was cold and unfeeling? It wasn't. It was more like…him giving up on his convictions, deciding that all this time, his rose-colored-glasses view of the world had been a joke.

It was that look that made me decide against a revenge scheme. No matter what he did to me, I was dead set against hurting him again.

And as much as I'd wanted to confront them, I still believed in Declan and me. We'd had more than a year together, a million memories that still managed to warm my heart, even when our relationship had soured. Back then, I was sure that we could turn things around if we both wanted it enough.

I pull myself out of bed and get ready for school. Kane is already outside when I hurry to my Jeep. It's warmer on this first day of March, and the piles of snow that have been hanging around seem to be liquefying and draining away. There are muddy patches of grass visible in the dingy snow. Without a word, I climb into my Jeep, but before I start the engine, I look at him.

"So they were sleeping together," I say. "But we didn't confront them."

He nods. "You didn't want to. You seemed convinced that things could go back to the way they were if we chilled. So we did."

"But they didn't go back, did they?"

"No," he says. "They got worse."

"Worse, how?"

"You and I cut ourselves off from each other. We agreed we'd put our energy into making things right. And we did that, for like two weeks." He shrugs. "You were so sure that he'd realize it was a mistake. You wanted him to confess and ask to start over."

"But he never did?"

He shakes his head.

"And then?"

Kane reaches over and starts the ignition. Even though it's warmer than past days, it's still cold, something I don't realize until the heat is pumping full blast at my face. "Come on, Hail."

"I still don't know why he died, Kane," I mutter. "And I know you've been lying to me. Hiding things from me."

"Why do you think? You'd just come out of an institution, Hailey. You were fragile. Did I want you reliving the fact that your boyfriend and your best friend did that to you? No. Did I want you to think that you took the picture that contributed to his suicide? No." His voice rises steadily. Finally, he stops and looks out the passenger window. "Why can't you see that everything I've done is for your own good?"

I bury my chin in my ski jacket and stare up at my house. Maybe I am due for a nervous breakdown. But I can't help feeling that not knowing will get me there faster than knowing.

"Look, Hailey," Kane says, his voice quieter. "Luisa and I had a talk last night. And we decided to start over. To wipe all away all the history. Again. Okay? But three strikes, and I'm out. So

I'm making this one worth it. I wanted you to know that while I've appreciated the ride, I'm going to get one with someone else from now on."

I look back at him. Five days. That's all it took. That's all it ever takes, right? Five days from pledging his undying love to me to blowing me off. He wasn't only leading Luisa on. He was leading me on too, and I was too stupid to realize it. It's such a fucking fine line between love and madness, and both Weeks boys have had me straddling it for far too long. I square my jaw and glare out the windshield. "Fine," I snap. "Then get out."

"Look, Hail. I—"

"GET OUT!" I shout, so loudly that it rattles the car.

He doesn't say a word. He pushes open the door. I throw the car in reverse and gun it out of the driveway before he's managed to clear the door. It smashes against him as I screech to a stop. He grips his sore arm and stares at me as I reach across and pull the passenger door closed. Then I floor the accelerator and pull out of the court, tires screeching, without another look in his direction.

25 Days Before

I'd slipped going down the trellis, falling back onto a prickly evergreen bush by the porch. It scraped my hands and face something awful, but I didn't feel it. I only realized it when I saw the dried blood on my sheets the following day. My reflection in the mirror was that of someone who'd gotten into a fight with a cat—and lost.

Over the night, I'd cried myself dry of tears. I blamed only myself. I'd started this.

And I knew I needed to finish it.

Even then, I thought I could find a way to reverse what had happened, to put life back the way it had been before. No, we were forever altered, but I thought that maybe I could still make my relationship right with Declan.

That morning, a Saturday, I texted Kane: **Can you come over?**

I barely ever texted Kane these days; usually, it was part of a group text. And though he was the type of guy who slept in on weekends, he responded at once: **What's up?**

I typed in: **I need to see you asap. Just come over.**

He didn't respond, but five minutes later, he appeared on my front stoop, knocking. I nearly mowed down my father, who was walking at a leisurely pace to answer the door. "I got it," I told him, nearly toppling him on the staircase in order to intercept Kane.

Kane was wearing an Eagles T-shirt, ball cap, and sweats despite the frigid weather and looked like he'd just woken up. I yanked him inside, afraid that Declan would see us. I'd already made enough of a mess with him thinking Kane and I had something going on. I didn't want to make the situation worse. When we were inside, he studied me in the darkened foyer. "What the hell happened to you?"

I motioned for him to be quiet and led him up to my bedroom. There, I found the photo I'd snapped and handed it to him. I hadn't actually looked at it as it developed, because I couldn't bring myself to. He studied it, squinting. "Wow. This captures it so well. What the hell is it?"

I grabbed the photo. Shit. I'd gotten mostly blinds in the picture, and only a blurred sliver of what might have been Declan's arm around Luisa's waist. But it was enough to bring back the horror of what I'd seen last night. I started to sob again.

"Whoa." Kane sat me down on the bed and waited for me to calm down.

I tried to explain, but my throat was choked with sobs. "I went to Declan's room last night. And…and he was with…Luisa…"

He stiffened. "What?"

I nodded. "They were…"

He stood up. "You're wrong. You have to be wrong."

"I'm not. I know what I saw. And I…" I covered my face with my hands. "There was no mistake, Kane. They were on his bed."

He ripped his phone out of his pocket and started to text.

"Wait, what are you doing?" I asked, alarmed.

"What do you think?" he snapped. "I'm going to ask her what she was doing last night. She told me she was still sick with that stomach bug, but I thought it was bullshit."

I grabbed the phone from him. "Wait." He tried to swipe it back, but I scooted off the bed. "Look. I don't…I don't want to confront him."

"What? Why the hell not? If Declan…and my girlfriend… I sure as hell want to confront him. It's got to be a mistake. Declan wouldn't…"

"Why not? You slept with his girlfriend."

Kane's face was red. Few things made him angry, but this qualified. I could tell he was running the past through his brain, trying to make sense of it. "If he did…I want to be the first to kick his ass."

"What about Luisa?"

"I wouldn't put it past her. Tell me you didn't see the way she looked at Declan. She was so jealous of you, it was practically coming out her ears. And after what we did…she saw her chance and she took it."

I put my head in my hands. "This is so horrible, Kane. I want it to stop. I want us all to go back to the way we were." Tears were still flowing from my eyes. "Please, Kane. I love Declan, more than anything. And I think he still loves me. There was something about Declan's face. I think he realized what he did was a mistake, even as it was happening."

"So?"

"So don't you see? They came together because of what *we* did. They aren't in love. It's…getting even. Now we're even. If we give them time, they'll come back to us. Isn't that what you want?"

He studied me. "Yeah. I guess." I handed the phone to him, and he stared at it. "So what do I say to her? Nothing?"

I nodded. "Yes. As hard as it is, we ride this out. And that means…"

He looked at me and pressed his lips together. We'd agreed, after the shit hit the fan about New Year's, that it was better if we lay low. Separated. It was hard, because our lives were so closely entwined, but we'd done our best. We still gravitated toward each other—without thinking, innocently ending up together—since he was the peanut butter to my jelly, the bacon to my eggs.

"I got it. I shouldn't be here." He pocketed his phone and strode to the window, looking across at his house. "What were they doing in there? Were they…" He threw up his hands. "You know, you're right. I don't want to know. My *stepbrother.*"

The images sifted through my mind again. I hadn't thought Declan was the type to get revenge, but it was possible. Love and rage make people do all kinds of things. "Well, we—"

"We did that before we even knew him. What Declan did… It's fucking worse. And you know it." He clenched his fists.

Because I'd lied to Declan for so long, I didn't quite see it that way. But I knew Kane couldn't be trusted to ride this out. When he got riled, watch out.

And he was definitely riled.

Saturday, March 2

My mother stops me at the door as I'm getting ready to leave for a shopping trip with Nina. "Are you okay?"

I nod. "I'm fine. Tired. But fine," I lie.

"Oh good," she says. "Because Mrs. Weeks might need a mother's helper on the weekends, what with baby Cooper. I thought it would be nice if you offered your time. Maybe you can make a little extra money."

I shake my head, but she isn't paying attention.

"That baby is supercute," she says with a smile. "She brought him over yesterday when they got back from the hospital. You should go over and see him."

That's the last thing I want to do. Declan's room is his nursery. And after my fight with Kane and nearly running over him with my Jeep, the Weeks house is the last place I want to be. I fudge an excuse as Nina's car pulls up our driveway.

When I climb in Nina's Honda Civic, she eyes me suspiciously. "So, I heard a little gossip through the grapevine."

I sink down low into the bucket seat. I wonder what piece of gossip she's talking about. Me nearly cutting myself open in gym a couple weeks ago? Me nearly getting into a catfight with Luisa over our dead boyfriend? Kane sleeping with me and then dumping me? None of it is anything I want repeated. "Can we shop and avoid the gossip?"

She pouts as she pulls out of my driveway. "But it's so juicy! And sad."

I heave a sigh. "All right, all right. What?"

"Maybe you already knew? Kane broke his shoulder on his throwing arm. And spring ball starts Monday."

I startle. "What? How?"

"He fell on some ice, he said." She shrugs. "All I know is that when Ethan came to pick him up yesterday morning for school, he had to drive him to the hospital. His shoulder is broken in three places."

I think back to when I drove out of the driveway like a bat out of hell, even before he'd gotten himself free of the Jeep.

Oh no.

I close my eyes. Holy hell. Had I...

Of course I had. And of course he wouldn't tell anyone what really happened. He's so worried about my mental state, and he wouldn't want Luisa to know he'd been talking to me. Guilt threatens to flood in, but I refuse to let it take a hold. After what he did to me last week, I refuse to care. I quickly change the subject.

"So, prom dresses. What are you looking for?"

I'd made plans with Nina to go prom-dress shopping, even though I knew I wouldn't be going. For years, prom dresses were a big topic of conversation, so it only seemed right for me to shop with her. The few times we'd shopped together, she'd come to really value my opinion, since I was honest and blunt.

"Oh, you know. Something to make Jav's tongue wag like a dog's over what he's missing," she says, smiling. "You are really so great for doing this with me, girl. I can't thank you enough. But you can still come to prom yourself, you know."

I scrunch my nose. Once upon a time, I'd imagined going to Declan's senior prom, and him coming back from his freshman year at college to escort me to mine. But the junior prom I'd gone to with Declan, the one where he'd sung me that goofy song, was enough. It had been a long time since I'd had prom dreams beyond that. "It's okay."

"But are you okay? I heard about your talk with Luisa."

I groaned. Yeah, and so had most of the school. "Did you know she was in love with Declan?" I ask.

She guns it through a yellow light that turns red the second we're through. "Oh. Um. I heard something about that. Yeah. Kind of a cluster, huh?"

"I guess I must have blocked it out. But they were seeing each other," I remark.

I study her for any reaction, but there is none. So she knew all along. Maybe I was the only one in the whole school who thought Declan was faithful to me. She says, "Do you really think he didn't kill himself?"

So, Crazy Hailey's wild conspiracy theories have reached the outside world. I have no doubt who's responsible for that. I told only one person my theory—Kane. And he told Luisa. And Luisa won't shut up, especially if it's damning gossip about me. "I don't know anymore. I mean, maybe he did. He had a lot of guilt, and I never knew it. He kept it inside. I obviously didn't know him as well as I thought."

"You knew him well, Hailey," she says. "He was a saint in a lot of ways. But even saints are human, you know? They make mistakes."

"But they atone for them."

"Who says he didn't?" she says. "Maybe that's what he thought he was doing when he got out the gun. Maybe he thought it was the only way to make up for what he'd done."

19 Days Before

I knew it wasn't working.

I knew Declan better than anyone. I knew he was a person of high morals, convictions. If he was cheating on me, it'd be eating away at him. He'd know it was wrong. If he had even one tiny bit of love left for me, he wouldn't be able to look at me without needing to confess. Eventually, he'd have to tell me everything. That was what I'd been counting on from the start.

And yet, he didn't.

The next two weeks went on, and it was like living in a fun-house mirror—normal, but distorted in so many ways. We spent time together, watching movies, studying together, doing the things we'd done before, but the mood was off. He'd hold my hand but wouldn't stroke my palm. He'd kiss me, but never with as much passion as before, as if his lips were there but his mind was somewhere else. He'd tell me he was busy, and I'd compare notes with Kane, and he'd say Luisa had bailed on him then too.

It was maddening.

It was a Saturday night, the first night we'd had alone. His parents were on a date night. Kane and Luisa were having dinner with her parents at their country club, so Declan and I were hanging out in his room. We kissed, hot and heavy, almost like before, but I couldn't stop think of Luisa being in that very spot. When I reached for his jeans and started to tug the button open, he stopped me.

And I lost it.

Because of course, he hadn't stopped *her*.

My hand froze in his. At that moment, I realized the folly of my plan. He was punishing me, playing with me, and I loved him so much that I could do nothing but let him twist me this way and that. I scooted away from him, toward the headboard of the bed, and started to sob.

"Hey," he said to me, almost back to the old, caring Declan I'd missed so much. He leaned back, watching me cry on his pillow. "What's wrong?"

I swabbed at my eyes. "You love me, right?"

"Of course," he said, but was there conviction in those words? It didn't seem so.

My fingers found the necklace, nestled in the hollow of my

throat. I touched it whenever I needed the assurance that Declan and I still meant something. I was doing it constantly now. The skin underneath was red and irritated. "And we're still going to be together. Forever?"

He just nodded and wiped a tear off my cheek. I wanted more reassurance. I needed it. But even if he had sworn up and down, any comfort he gave me wouldn't be enough. "What's the problem?"

I shrugged. "Nothing. I'm stressed, I guess. College worries, you know."

He smiled. "Been there." He kissed my forehead, then ran a finger over the worry lines there. It felt nice, the kind of touch I'd craved and been starved of lately. "Do you want some Excedrin? Something to drink?"

I nodded, lapping up the concern like an abandoned puppy that was offered a treat. "Thanks."

He started to get up, then stopped, opened his mouth, then clamped it shut again. Then he said, "Hey. I had something I wanted to talk to you about."

I looked at him, hopeful. "Yes?"

He said, "Hailey. I..." He paused as if he wasn't sure how to phrase it. Then he said, quickly, "I wanted to know if you would go to prom with me."

The smile broke out on my face immediately, huge and almost painful. I hadn't used those muscles much in the past month.

"Yes. Yes!" I dove for him, hugging him hard. I kissed him, unable to wipe that stupid grin off my face.

"Cool." He sprang off the bed. "Back in a minute."

I sat up, adjusting my bra and closing the clasp. As happy as I was, it only took another minute before I felt dirty, gross, sitting in the same spot where I'd seen him with Luisa. He'd invited me to prom, but suddenly I felt like a consolation prize. He'd had time to confess, but one thing was clear...he didn't want to. Not only that, he and Luisa had been MIA yesterday. He was still seeing her.

My eyes trailed to his phone, sitting on the night table. I grabbed it, opened it, and found his texts. Sure enough, he'd been texting with Luisa. It said "L", but it didn't take a genius to crack that code. The last message was from a few hours ago. I opened it and read the screen:

January 27, 9:58 PM

Meet you there at 10:30

Can't wait :)

January 28, 4:50 PM

Have fun with your girl ;)

Rather be with you

The whole time I was reading, I'd been pulling on a lock of my hair and didn't realize until I'd torn it from my scalp. It had taken a little chunk of skin too. I stared at the strands, then held them over carpet and let them fall to floor.

Rather be with you.

He was going to prom with me, and yet he'd rather be with her.

I heard him coming up the stairs. I'd wanted to read more, but I quickly placed the phone on the night table, and grabbed the closest book, which happened to be his Bible.

He was surprised to see me reading it, since I'd shied away from it before. He set two Cokes on the dresser and handed me a couple of green pills. "What are you doing?"

I scanned the page. He'd outlined some of the words in yellow, but I didn't see those. Somehow, the first words I read were these:

Do you not know that the unrighteous will not inherit the kingdom of God? Do not be deceived; neither the immoral, nor idolaters, nor adulterers, nor sexual perverts, nor thieves, nor the greedy, nor drunkards, nor revilers, nor robbers will inherit the kingdom of God.

"Nothing," I said, feeling dizzy, drained. *Rather be with you.* Those two pills were like putting a bandage on cancer.

I took them anyway. When he leaned over to give them to me, he touched my forehead and brought back blood on the pad of his finger. "What the..."

I grabbed a tissue, blotting the sore, which didn't even hurt compared to everything else that was wrong with me. I replied lifelessly, "Nothing."

"Wow," he said, sitting down on the antique rocking chair in the corner of the room, far away from me. "You *are* stressed out."

Stress. Right. If that was all it was, I'd have been happy. But I hadn't even had a chance to think about college. I couldn't, not with my social life going to pot. My mother had strategically placed brochures for Penn State in places around the house where I'd find them, but all I could think was that as much as he promised we were forever, Declan had started moving away from me. In another year, he'd be in Philadelphia, and I'd be at home. Everything I'd done to draw him toward me had only succeeded in pushing him further away.

We didn't kiss again after that. Didn't even touch. I felt like a diversion, like someone he was passing time with when he really wanted to be with someone else. He only talked about UPenn and how acceptances should be coming in another month or so. Where before I'd imagined walking the tree-lined campus with him, hand in hand, now I imagined him walking with Luisa. The more he talked, the sicker I felt, as though I was no longer a part of his future. As if my future, once so set in stone, had become a big, terrifying question mark.

If I couldn't trust Declan to be honest with me, who could I trust?

When he excused himself to use the bathroom, I found a purple highlighter in my backpack and marked those sentences, thickly and angrily. Then I stuck the red ribbon bookmark in the page and laid the Bible on his pillow, so that he wouldn't be able to escape those damning words, no matter how hard he tried.

Tuesday, March 5

I haven't slept in days. Not since I discovered what a cheating liar I was. I can't help thinking that Luisa was right: I am responsible for Declan's death.

Juliet watches me silently as I sit in the blue chair in her office. I take a bottle of Poland Spring, drink, and say, "I don't have very much to say today."

"You don't? You missed last week."

It's not that I don't have things to say. I don't have the energy to say them. "Everything's fine. Good. I mean, I even went shopping this weekend. For prom dresses."

She stares at me with narrowed eyes as if she doesn't believe me. "That's great. You're going to the prom?"

"Oh. No. I'm... You know. Moving on. Like I should be. Right?"

I thought that was the correct answer, but from the way she's looking at me, it's not.

"Yes. But what brought this about?" She flips through pages on her clipboard. "Last time we met, you were having some concerns about Declan's death."

I nod. "I don't have them anymore. He killed himself."

She seems surprised by my progress. She taps her pen on her pad. "And what brought you to that conclusion?"

Do I have to go into it? I'm not sure I can. Instead, I say, "I went through the box."

"The box of things his mother gave you? So you found it therapeutic?"

I nod. She seems pleased, as though her suggestion has me on the path to recovery, and if she wants to think that, fine. I'm happy to increase her self-worth the way she thinks she's increasing mine. "I found mementos from things he did with my best friend. My ex-best friend. And it made me remember things about him. He was cheating on me."

"With"—she flips back some pages—"Luisa?"

"Yes. He had this whole secret life I knew nothing about, and so I guess I didn't know him well. I spoke to his priest, and he told me that Declan had stopped going to church, and that he was one to harbor guilt and not let it out. Maybe he was suicidal. I can't know what was going through his head, because I didn't know him." I swallow, pushing away memories that will only have me sobbing again.

"And?"

"And what? It hurts. But part of me feels like a weight has been lifted off me. I'd built him up in my head, thought he was so perfect. I was worried I wasn't good enough for him. Now? I don't know. It helps to know he was human."

She smiles. "Well, that's encouraging."

"So, yes," I say. "I'm not the person who knew him best. I didn't know that he had a vengeful side. That he could sleep with someone to get even, then lie straight to my face about it."

"You think that's what he did?"

I nod. "I know it. He couldn't have cared about Luisa. Please. She told me she thought it's my fault he died."

"You spoke to her?"

I nodded again. Wow, it turns out, a lot *has* happened since I last spoke to Juliet. "Yes. I guess she meant he was so full of guilt over hurting me. And I..." I blush sheepishly. "I didn't make it easy for him. I highlighted quotes in his Bible."

"You did?" She gives me a reproachful look. "But that alone wouldn't make Declan..."

"No, but maybe there were a thousand little things I didn't know about that all contributed. Luisa would know. She was spending more time with him. And if she's blaming me, something tells me she's probably covering for herself. Maybe she pressured him to end things with me."

"You think?"

"I know the way she pushed Kane. She was relentless. He could only take her in small doses."

"So you think Declan's relationship with Luisa was his undoing?"

"She has this subtle way about her. She comes across as all rainbows and sunshine, but she can be lethal."

Juliet purses her lips. "And where is Luisa now?"

"Terrorizing Kane, once again. She's got a magnet for him. They made up. They're together."

"And how do you feel about that?"

I shrug. "I don't have any feelings about that. Luisa never lets anything touch her. She comes out of every crisis prettier and shinier than she was going in."

"You sound bitter."

"Well, considering I'm still here, a year later...talking to you. I wish I had her resiliency."

Juliet checks her notes and says, "It concerns me that you don't have a best friend to lean on anymore. I suppose you still have Kane, and—"

I shake my head. I hadn't seen him since Friday, but everyone was talking about his broken shoulder. Word on the street was that he was pissed. Baseball is his life, and he'd been waiting all winter for it to start up again. And who knows if it'll affect his chance at getting into college? He probably wants to kill me.

"No. That's kind of… No. You see, we… He and I…"

She's staring at me, and I can't say it. Talk about going around in circles, banging my head against the wall. "Seems like you have a lot to say to me today," Juliet comments.

I sigh. "It was a mistake. In the end, Kane chose Luisa over me. And that's all. Like I said, prettier and shinier. I don't want to talk about that. I'm okay. Really."

I push the corners of my lips into a smile to prove it.

"All right," she says, closing her notebook. "You're moving on, and that's important. Are you finding something to hitch your wagon to that isn't part of the past?"

"Like…?"

"College, trade school…" she suggests. "Your life. You're graduating in three months, which isn't long."

I hadn't thought of college at all, honestly, until this weekend. My parents were simply happy with me graduating from high school in some capacity. Taking baby steps. But Nina's acceptances were starting to come in, and she was trying to decide between Moravian and Cedar Crest. And, for the first time, my mind had started to trail to my future. My after.

Because there would be an after. Before, I'd thought that with Declan gone, my life might as well end. But it hasn't. I'm still here. And I will be here, whether I make sense of his death or not.

Declan's death had permanently shattered the six, but soon

its pieces would be scattered all over the country. I can write my own story from here on out, not as Declan's girlfriend, but as whomever I wanted to be.

"I am thinking of it," I announce. "I might enroll in community college."

Juliet smiles, and I can tell I've pleased her. "Good for you, Hailey. Good for you."

12 Days Before

I had just enough time.

Declan had a crap locker assignment. His was all the way down in no-man's-land, in the band wing, away from all of his classes. He didn't even take band, so he'd always make it to class with seconds to spare. Since he had too many books to lug them all around all day, I'd rarely see him between classes unless he was sprinting somewhere.

I asked for a nurse's pass during the last five minutes of geometry so I could make sure no one would see me. When I got past the nurse's office, I booked it double time into the music wing just as the bell rang.

I should have had the time.

But I couldn't find the photograph in my purse. I had one of those purses with fifteen zippers, and couldn't remember where I'd put it. Once I found it, I slid it into the slats at the top of his locker. Students started streaming down the hall toward me.

I'd taken three steps when I saw Declan rushing, doing his usual four-minute between-class sprint.

He saw me at once, and slowed. My palms slicked. I swallowed.

"Hey," he said. "What are you doing here?"

"I came to see Nurse Fielding," I said. "Female problem."

Usually, the female thing got guys to stop asking questions. And it worked with Declan too. But I could tell those big, brilliant cogs in his mind were working, because the nurse's office was on the other side of the band wing. Meaning, I'd have no reason to come down this far, unless I'd been stopping at his locker. He didn't ask about that, though. "Are you feeling all right?"

I nodded and pointed to the water fountain behind me. "Yeah. Had some water. And now I feel better."

My face was burning with heat. I had the world's most pathetic poker face. I knew he must have seen the Bible. He must have known that I'd outlined those passages. All I wanted was for him to acknowledge that I knew. To say something, so I wouldn't have to.

But he said absolutely nothing. He was content to let me twist in the wind. He was happy not to confess, or maybe he didn't care to, as if I didn't matter enough to him.

"Cool," he said, starting to pick up his pace. "See you later?"

"Yeah."

Then he rounded the corner and disappeared.

I kicked a locker, clenching my fists so tightly that my

fingernails dug into the skin of my palms, making them bleed. When I went to my class—ten minutes late, but who cared?—I sent a text to Kane, as my teacher was writing out my detention slip: **Did Luisa say anything to you?**

He texted back: **No**

I'd had enough time to send one more text as my teacher finished writing. I held the phone under my desk and jabbed: **Are you going to tell her you know?**

As I walked to detention, I got the message from him: **No**

I stood there in the deserted hallway, my thumbs hovering over the keypad. I felt desperate, out of control, a volcano ready to blow its top off, but I didn't know what would make me feel better. Well, I did know, but I knew that wasn't possible. And it killed me.

A second later, he came back with: **I have to lift after school. Meet me outside the gym after? Like 6?**

It was a Friday. I knew spring ball would be starting, and Kane would be working off the past couple months of heavy partying and his penchant for eating an entire pizza by himself. Not that Kane ever showed a hint of imperfection. At least he had something to keep his mind off his cheating girlfriend. I'd given up dance for my junior year, never having made it to soloist, so I had absolutely nothing to occupy the time.

When six o'clock rolled around, the school was deserted. I sat on the floor of the hallway outside the locker room. I'd been there for the past hour. I told myself I'd tackle my geometry homework, but I hadn't cracked the book. I simply sat there, cross-legged, back against the wall, replaying every moment I'd had with Declan until I was beyond madness.

When Kane finally opened the door and came out, carrying the scent of soap from his recent shower, my eyes were so swollen from crying that I couldn't even see him.

"Wow," he said, slinking down next to me. "Drama much?"

I tried to talk, but I couldn't. I sucked in a breath that did nothing to help me calm down. Then I grabbed my chest. "I can't breathe," I sobbed. "Kane…I can't breathe."

He put an arm around me and let me cry into his shoulder, making quiet shushing noises to get me to calm down, but my heart was going a million miles an hour and I felt like it might explode.

"He's not coming back. I can't do this," I said into the warm dampness of his sweatshirt hood.

"I know," he said.

I'm not sure how I ended up in the passenger seat of my Jeep in the empty lot of the high school. When he slid into the driver's seat, he was holding the keys, but I couldn't remember giving them to him. He looked at me and said, "You're going to be okay."

Except I felt as though my heart was so scarred, it would never heal. Still, sometime during the walk to the Jeep, I'd stopped feeling sorry. Now, my blood was boiling. I leaned over the console, without hesitation, and kissed him, hard.

"You never kissed me," I said, humiliation creeping in as I realized what I'd done. "That first time. And I was too drunk to remember the second."

The look of surprise that flashed on his face soon dissolved as he reached a hand around my neck, pulling me close to him again. We kissed, ravenously. It turned out, while those first fumblings when we were fifteen had been nothing worth writing home about, kissing him hit me in all the right places. For the first time that year, I felt more than the fear of losing the best thing that had ever happened to me. No wonder Declan hated me. If it had been this good on New Year's, then it must have been obvious how much I enjoyed it.

We ended up in the cramped back seat of my Jeep, half-clothed, doing what we shouldn't have, considering we were dating other people. All the while, he kept whispering that we were going to be okay, that I'd survive this. Even if it didn't feel real, it felt right. And the hurting stopped, briefly, which was the best that I could hope for.

Wednesday, March 6

When I stepped out of my Jeep after school, I looked across the street at the Weeks place. Mrs. Weeks's SUV was in the driveway.

Kane hadn't been at school. I'd only seen him once since Friday, and that was out my bedroom window, when he got into his father's truck. He was wearing a sling on his arm and a baseball cap on his head, so I couldn't see his face. I imagine he was still pissed at me. I hadn't had the guts to text him.

Taking a breath, I throw my backpack on the front stoop of my house and jog over to theirs. I knock on the door, in case the baby's sleeping. Mrs. Weeks answers a moment later. "Hailey," she says, smiling. "How are you?"

"Good. I—"

I don't have time to explain. She motions me inside, and I follow her up the stairs. By time we get to the end of the hall, my heart is in my throat. But I swallow it down. She turns to me. "Are you going to be okay?"

I nod.

And I go inside.

They painted the room. It's a mint-green color, and there are cartoon turtles all over the walls. I smell baby powder. The crib and matching furniture is new, white wicker. They didn't change out the carpet, though, and there are impressions where his bed frame had been. I hover in the doorway, thinking of him sitting there, the first time we met, playing that silly song for me on his guitar.

Then I take a step inside. I feel warm, dizzy as I peer into the crib, meeting Mr. Cooper Weeks for the first time. Declan's little brother. He's wrapped tight in a green blanket, but his arms are free, raised like a goalpost. Thick eyelashes, chubby cheeks. Long, pink fingers, the kind I could see playing an instrument.

But what strikes me most are the eyebrows. The very familiar arch.

"Oh my gosh," I breathe. "He's beautiful."

"So you came to see my little brother, not me?" someone whispers from the door. "I'm beautiful too."

We turn to see Kane standing in the doorway. He's barefoot and bare-chested, wearing the sling and a pair of sweatpants. Mrs. Weeks shushes him and ushers us out the door.

Making jokes? So he isn't angry at me? And here, if the roles had been reversed, I'd be livid.

When Mrs. Weeks closes the nursery door on us, leaving us alone in the hallway, I say, "I'm so sorry."

"You should be." Then he smirks. "I get it. I'm an asshole."

"No, you're not. All the things you did to protect me. You are definitely not an asshole."

He seems surprised. "What are you talking about?"

"I remembered more. Even before Declan died, I was falling apart."

"Yeah, you were. He wasn't very nice to you, Hailey. Especially at the end there." He shrugs. "But I've done stupid things in the name of love too. So I get it."

"You kept me together." I shrug. "So anyway, thanks. When are you coming back to school?"

"Tomorrow." He motions me toward his room. It's hot and stuffy in there, as if he's been marinating in his bed for the past five days. He shows me a letter with a red and gold logo on it. It takes me a minute to recognize it as FSU—Florida State University. Kane never talked about college much, but when he did, it was Florida, Florida, Florida. I scan the letter and see the word "Congratulations." I raise my eyebrow.

He grins. "I may be an asshole, but I'm also going to be a Seminole."

241

No wonder he's happy. "No way!"

"I know. I can't believe they want me, either." He scans the letter again. "And Luisa will be in Miami, so…" He stops and bows his head sheepishly, as if he just realized who he's talking to and wishes he could take it back. "It's good."

"Oh, about that. Listen. I get your thing with Luisa. I get that you're trying to start fresh, and I don't want to get in the way of that." I suck in a breath. "So you don't have to keep coming to my rescue anymore, okay?"

He sets the letter down. "I don't—"

"I need to start doing that for myself. Everyone else is moving forward, and I'm stuck in the past. I need to grow up and take responsibility for my future."

He nods. "Yeah. All right."

I start to jog down the stairs, feeling for the first time as if I'm finally growing up and stepping off that hamster wheel. Like maybe I'll be okay.

"Wait," he says when I'm nearly at the bottom. I turn back. "Still friends, right?"

I smile at him. "Always."

9 Days Before

I tried to see him over the weekend. I texted, asking if he wanted to do something. I went to his house, but he wasn't home. I'd spent most of that weekend thinking of plans to get closer to him. Then I took one of my stuffed animals, christened it Luisa, and did some voodoo on it with a very sharp sewing needle.

In the morning, a plan had solidified in my head. I never drove Declan to school anymore, since he usually took the bus to get there early for Science Club. But I had the idea that I would make an excuse to take the early bus too.

When I saw him leave the house—so ridiculously early that it was still black as night outside—I rushed out, screen door banging behind me, chasing after him. I nearly slipped on the ice, trying to catch up to him. "Hey," I said, out of breath when I fell in stride on the sidewalk next to him. "Hi."

"Hey," he said, digging his hands deep into the pockets of the inadequately light corduroy jacket he was wearing. He didn't look at me. "Your Jeep okay?"

"It's been making a sound."

He let out a laugh. "It's older than shit. It makes a lot of sounds. Can you be more specific?"

I didn't want to talk about my fucking car, especially since there was nothing wrong with it. Ignoring him, I said, "Science Club today?"

He nodded.

"What are you working on?"

"Nothing that would interest you," he said with a shrug, which made me curse all the times I'd told him I didn't want to hear him explain the ins and outs of his latest creation.

The conversation faltered, mostly because it was so one-sided anyway. "So how was your weekend?"

We got to the edge of the development. He turned and looked at me. "So why are you here again?"

I pointed toward Fox Court. "My…Jeep…"

It wasn't very convincing. The bus bumped toward us, and he let me on first. It was empty. When I sat down in the middle of the bus, he slipped past me toward the very back. Sighing, I pulled my bag out of the seat I'd selected and joined him. He looked up at me as if he'd been cornered, then took a notebook out of his bag. "Sorry," he said when I opened my mouth to ask him another question. He pointed at the notebook page, which was scattered with intimidating equations. "I've got to study."

"Okay," I said, sinking down into my seat. This was ridiculous. He usually avoided confrontation. I was his girlfriend. He couldn't ignore me forever, thinking I'd slink away without an explanation.

When the bus pulled into the U-shaped drive in front of the school, Declan quietly put his things into his bag and started past me once again without another word. I'd had enough. I jumped to my feet. "Okay, enough, Declan. Tell me," I shouted down the aisle. He turned. The sun had started to rise, so I could see that his eyes were tired. "Are we done?"

He looked at me and then at the bus driver. "Not here."

And he walked off.

Clenching my fists, I raced after him. "Then where? Tell me where you'll talk to me, because I can't seem to find a place."

He stopped. Then, shrugging, he motioned for me to follow him. The lights in the school were on, but it was pretty quiet this early in the morning. I followed him to the closest empty classroom, and he closed the door. He dropped his heavy backpack at his feet and stared at me blankly. "What?"

What. He said it just like that, as if he had no idea. "Don't you have something to tell me?"

He did something I'd never heard him do before—he let out a bitter laugh. "Are you serious, Hailey?"

"Yeah."

"Why don't we start with what you had to tell me? Because that happened first."

I swallow. "Yes, but it happened before you and I met, so there was nothing to tell."

A smile spreads over his face, but it's not a happy one. It's ironic and pained. "Hailey. I don't care that it happened. I care that you never told me that you'd slept with my stepbrother. You never told me. All those times we talked about our first time, and you simply went along with it. You really think I'd care if you had sex before?"

I nodded. "Yes, because—"

He shook his head. "No. It wouldn't have mattered. I wouldn't have cared if you slept with a thousand people before me, if I thought you were being honest with me."

"But…"

"You need to stop. With the pictures. With whatever you're doing. Just stop," he said, running his hands through his hair. "Because I can't take it. I loved you so much, Hailey."

Loved. Past tense.

My heart broke open. It spilled all over that classroom.

And he didn't care.

"So much, I would've done anything for you. I would've gotten past any of your flaws." He gazed at me as he spoke, his words trembling in his throat, and I remembered how he could gaze at me with a love so intense it could put my pieces back together. Now, his stare was so cold I felt myself ripping at the seams. "But you lied to me *the whole time*. For a whole year. And I can't get past that. No matter what you say, it's too late."

He picked up his bag and started to leave. I tried to block the door, but I wasn't fast enough, and I couldn't think of anything to say. He had every right to hate me. I didn't have to ask him if we were over. I knew the answer. "You're with Luisa, then."

"Yeah," he said. "I am."

And he walked away, leaving me alone and in a thousand pieces that would never come back together the same way again.

Friday, June 14

Early congratulations to me, *I think, licking chocolate*
icing off the doughnut I'd bought from Yum Yum Donut Shop.

I page through my Facebook feed, reading all the congratulations and "This is the first day of the rest of our lives!" crap. I
should be donning my cap and gown to say goodbye to Deer Hills
High with them. Unfortunately, due to my Shady Harbor stay, I'm
two classes short of graduating, which I'll remedy this summer.

I stop on Nina's feed, where there's a picture of the happy
graduating couple. Javier's wearing his green gown and grinning,
but under the gown, I can only see his spindly, hairy ankles. It
looks like he's not wearing a stitch of clothing, which is probably
why Nina is frowning in the picture. I smile.

On Kane's feed is a picture of Luisa, wearing a sultry white
dress, cap, and her valedictorian honors sash and National Honor
Society cord. She's holding the cap on her head and laughing with

all her teeth, and it's an amazing picture because it makes her look practically ethereal. He'd written: *My beautiful girl <3. So proud.*

I check the time. It's nearly seven.

My destination closes at eight. When I finish my doughnut, I kiss my mom goodbye and head out in my Jeep. When I get to the campus of Bucks County Community College, most of the cars are clearing out. The registrar is almost empty. I approach the desk, and an elderly lady with glasses smiles at me. "Can I help you?"

I take out my transcript. "I applied online for the fall semester but was hoping to take some enrichment courses this summer," I say. "Can you help me?"

"Oh, of course. What are you looking to take?"

"English literature," I say as the door behind me opens. The woman lays out a rather long-looking form and outlines the sections I need to complete. I start to fill it out as someone sets their elbows on the counter next to me.

"I need to add a class, please," a deep, low voice says.

I look up into two of the bluest eyes I've ever seen. He's studying the form I'm filling out. "New student, Hailey?"

I stare at him. How does he know my name?

He must read my mind, because he points to the form. Then he grins and extends a hand. "I'm Silas."

I shake it. "Yes, I'm new."

He lifts his bag onto his shoulder. "Need someone to show you around?"

I shake my head. "No, I'm good. Thanks."

"Here we go, English Literature," the woman behind the counter says, handing me another paper. And just like that, I'm enrolled in my first college-level class.

"English Lit? Seriously?" Silas asks, holding a Jane Austen book. "That's the class I'm adding."

I smile.

"It's fate," he says.

And maybe it is.

7 Days Before

Deer Hills was like a minefield. Before, I'd barely ever see Luisa or Declan in the hallway, but now I started seeing them all the time. The two of them didn't flaunt their relationship with massive PDAs. Neither of them was like that, unlike Kane, who'd have his hands all over her. But they did hold hands. Once I came around the corner and saw them staring into each other's eyes, not even speaking. They looked deep, meaningful, like a picture postcard. Where I used to think Kane and Luisa were enviable as a couple?

It was nothing compared to this.

They were both brilliant. They were both talented. It almost seemed as though Kane and I were roadblocks on their path to true love.

"Well," Kane said to me one day, coming up behind me and

resting an arm against the locker besides mine. "I feel like shit. How about you?"

"Same," I muttered, following his line of vision to where Luisa and Declan were walking down the hall, holding hands. I slammed my locker without thinking and almost snagged my finger. "You spoke to him?"

He shrugged. "I told you. He said we're not brothers anymore. And I said that was fine with me."

"How can you live under the same roof like that?"

"Because I know something he doesn't know."

"Which is?"

"That she may look like she's with him, but *I* was the one she was drunk-texting last night." He held out his phone triumphantly.

"What?" I grabbed his phone and scanned the messages. It was all a lot of bullshit, like "What are you up to/Nothing, what are you up to?" at first, but then it got more personal. The time stamp on it was after one in the morning, and she admitted she'd been taking sips of the wine her mother had left in the fridge. Kane was his usual distant self, and it was clear she'd fallen for it hook, line, and sinker, because at the end, she'd typed, "I miss you," and he hadn't responded.

God, he was a champion.

I wished Declan had drunk-texted me. Not like that would ever happen, since he didn't drink. But I wanted some signal, any signal, that he still thought about me. As it was, he hadn't even looked at me. No, I'd looked at him enough for the both of us, and not only that, but I felt bad for him. That's how much I loved him. I felt bad that Luisa was playing him, and he didn't know. I wanted to warn him. "Maybe I should tell him."

Sensing my desperation, Kane wrapped a hand around my upper arm. "Hailey. Don't. Stand strong. Don't get pulled back in."

That's easy to say when you're standing at the edge. I'd already slipped and was falling, headfirst, no idea if there was even a bottom to land on.

I felt the tears welling in my eyes for the thousandth time that week. I watched Declan as he tucked a strand of blond hair behind Luisa's ear and stroked her cheek. I could almost feel his callused, gentle Californian finger stroking my cheek. "But... does he even think about me, you think?"

"I'm sure he does," Kane said, which was too vague for me.

I wanted to *know*. I didn't want to feel like Declan had left me in the dust to rot. I wanted to know he cared. Even a little bit. "You think so?"

Kane nodded. "Yeah. He does. Give him time, okay? It sucks now, you're right. But he loves you. So give him his space. All right?"

I watched as Luisa slammed her locker door and they started to walk away, pinkies intertwined. Giving him space? Easier said than done.

Thursday, July 4

Someone's setting off fireworks outside.

I don't have to look to know who it is. People always seem to fall in one camp or the other when it comes to DIY fireworks, and while I was always in the Hate camp, Kane had always been in the Worth-It-Even-If-I-Blow-Myself-Up camp.

I look at the latest text from Silas and smile. **Can't believe you didn't like it. Do you have no heart?**

He's talking about Harry Potter. None of the novels are part of our English Lit class, and yet he's Hufflepuff forever and insists that the books should be a part of the curriculum. I'd read the first one, but ugh, it wasn't the easiest to slog through. I've definitely liked other books better. When I told him that, he said, *Well, it was nice talking to you, but we can't be friends anymore.*

But I think we've become more than that. It's been three weeks, and we've been texting a lot. He's into literature, writing, and reading the way that Declan was into all things science and engineering. Silas'd wanted to go to a four-year college, even got accepted to Penn State, but he thought he could save money by doing his first two years at community college and then transferring. We haven't kissed, haven't really touched, funny enough.

But I'm starting to wonder what it would be like to.

The fireworks are going off like crazy around here, I type after tenting our latest assigned reading on my stomach. *Sense and Sensibility*. We'd started by comparing observations about the books, but now we text about everything.

Same here. Giving up for tonight and joining the festivities. Talk later?

I text back: **Yep. Have fun.**

As I hit Send, I hear Kane's whooping, followed by a loud *whizz-pop*. I tilt the blinds. He's crouched alone in the center of the court, a bunch of spent firework debris all around him. From what I can see, he has a full crate of them. I push open the window and shout, "Keep it down out here!"

He gives me both fingers and says, "It's the Fourth of July! Have some patriotism!"

I decide to go down and watch the show, which may or may not include him blowing a limb off. It's only when I get outside that I see Luisa is sitting on the steps to his house, watching, her fingers in her ears. "Hey," she calls to me.

I haven't talked to her since before school let out, and even then, it was a forgettable exchange, like nice-weather-we're-having. But she hasn't scowled at me, so I guess we're cool. I wave and sit on my steps to watch. She gets up, comes over to me, and sits beside me, offering a bag of microwave popcorn. I take a handful. "How are you?" she asks.

"Fine. You? I hear you're off to college soon."

She smiles. "Miami."

"That's good. Close to Kane, at least."

She chews on some popcorn and shakes her head. "He told you that? Moron. It's an eight-hour drive. He'll be all the way across the state from me."

Well, that's Kane. To Kane, an eight-hour drive is a minor detail. "Should be nice, though."

"Yeah. I'm excited." She's wearing a little sundress, and she hugs her bare knees to herself. She's not one to get sunburns, but all the weekends going to the beach with Kane have given her a bit of a tan. "So are you going to school?"

"Just community college for now. I'll transfer to four-year in two years, maybe," I say.

Kane lets off another one, which is more of a noisemaker than anything else. It soars up into the sky, and we keep waiting for the pretty bloom of light, but nothing happens except an enormous pop that makes both of us jump. Kane fist-pumps, like it's excellent. Luisa looks at me and rolls her eyes.

"I wanted to tell you, before I left," she says, leaning forward. "I didn't mean what I said. It wasn't your fault."

I wave her away. "It's okay."

"He loved us both," she says quietly. "And he felt like no matter what choice he made, he was betraying someone. He hated letting people down. It made him feel so guilty."

A kernel of corn is caught in my throat, so I cough it loose, turning her words over. Yes, he felt guilt deeply, though something about that doesn't seem quite right. After all this time, it also doesn't feel right to argue. I nod as a memory comes to me. Me and Declan, in my bedroom.

She continues: "I remember the last thing he told me, the night before he died. He wasn't happy. He told me wished he'd never moved here. He felt like everyone had turned against him. I told him it'd be better in college, but he was still upset. I only wish I'd known how upset he was."

He'd never told me that. No, whenever we spoke about him moving here, he'd said it was the best thing that ever happened to him, for the sole reason that it brought us together.

But water under the bridge. I may never know why he killed himself, but I think I can live with myself.

We watch the rest of the fireworks explode in the air without talking. Some of them are actually worth the effort Kane puts in. By the time he's done, it's getting chilly, so I say I'll see them around and go back inside.

The Day Before

That week, I cried rivers.

In school, everyone was excited about either one of two things: Valentine's Day or the approaching snowstorm. I couldn't get excited about any of it. I'd foolishly handed in my stupid Valentine's note to the Key Club a month earlier, and I was told by the board that there was no way I could get it back. I was embarrassed enough by that, but even more embarrassed by the fact that I'd made a holiday I'd previously deemed stupid mean so much. Just because of a damn guy. How dumb could I be?

I never talked to Declan anymore. Instead, I stalked his social media. Where he used to clog his feed with pictures of us, now the pictures were gone. He filled his feed with mundane and infrequent posts about his life. There was one from two weeks ago that said, *Hello, February.* And the most recent had been posted that day. *Wawa packed with people getting bread and milk. Couldn't get gas.*

I'd stared at that tweet for an hour, almost as if it was a code, and cracking it would reveal that he missed me. Of course, it didn't.

I trudged home, hoping for a big storm, a really big one that would keep us snowbound until this crappy winter ended. The meteorologists said we were right on the cusp, so it could be a big storm, but there were no promises. I crept into my room, thinking that with my luck, I'd be forced to endure another Valentine's Day alone. I'd never cared much before, but now it seemed so much worse because I'd had all these expectations for me and Declan.

I was too sad to do my homework. After dinner, I got into my pajamas and crawled into bed. But I tossed and turned. Then I nearly fell out of it when I turned toward my window and saw a dark form sitting on the overhang of our porch, a ghostly pale face illuminated by the moonlight.

When it knocked, I startled again. It was Declan.

I ran to slide open the window. We didn't have a trellis. "How did you...?" I asked him, looking down.

"Gutter," he said, climbing inside. I'd seen him in school only briefly, and he'd been wearing the same clothes: jeans and his corduroy jacket. "And I think I killed that bush down there."

"It's okay," I told him. He had a scrape from one of the branches on his cheek. It was bleeding. I grabbed a tissue and held it up to his cheek. He took it, as if he was embarrassed to have me help him. "Is everything okay?"

"No," he said. "It's all wrong. And for the past few weeks I've been trying to figure out why. I kept avoiding the obvious answer, but I can't anymore. It's clearly the only thing that will make things right."

"What?"

"I miss you," he said.

My mouth hung open.

"Listen. I don't care what you did. I get it. If you really loved being with Kane, you would have been with him. But you weren't, and there's a reason for that. It's because you belong with me. All I care about is what happens from this day on. And if you feel the same way, and if we both promise not to make the same mistakes, there's no reason it can't work, right?"

"But, Luisa—"

"That's what I'm telling you. I'm breaking up with her. All I was doing, and all I would ever do for the rest of my life, is compare girls to you. You're my girl, Hailey. You fit with me."

He took my hand. His were like ice, as if he'd walked home from Luisa's while thinking about that. I couldn't speak. It was everything I'd wished he would give to me, and maybe that's why it scared me so much.

"Let's do something. Can you come with me?" he asked.

"It's the middle of the night," I said. But I would've gone anywhere with him.

We managed to creep downstairs, into the backyard to the broken-down pirate's ship. We climbed up into the clubhouse, even though it was clumped with old snow. He said, "Remember that night?"

Of course I did. The night we kissed for the first time.

I wanted to go back. I wanted to start again. "If I could, I would have told you everything, Declan," I said to him. "I promise."

"I know," he said, wrapping an arm around me to ward off the cold. "I know."

Monday, July 8

MORNING

Finished!

The text comes in at seven in the morning. I rip the pillow off my head and groan as the bright summer light assaults my eyes. Then I look at my phone and smile.

I type in: **Scumbag. I'm still on page 280.**

Home stretch. Text me after you read the thrilling conclusion.

I check my phone again to make sure I hadn't read the time wrong. No, it seriously is only seven in the morning on a summer Monday. Being up this early is probably against the law in some cultures. **It's too early. My mind doesn't process anything until 9 at the earliest.**

Text me at 9:45.

Sorry. Have to work today.

I kick out of bed, get dressed in my summer uniform of jean shorts and a tank, and braid my hair. After breakfast, I head across the street to the Weeks house, where I've been acting as mother's helper to Mrs. Weeks for the last few days.

"Hello, little Mr. Cooper," I say to the smiling infant in the bouncy seat, giving the seat a nudge so that the lights and music above will go on. He squeals with glee.

"Are you sure you're okay, staying here with me?" Mrs. Weeks calls as she cleans out bottles in the kitchen. "Kane and the others are going to Long Beach Island for the day. I don't want you to miss out on summer on account of me."

"No, I'm good," I tell her. I wasn't invited, not that I would've gone anyway. I know that everyone's going their separate ways at the end of August, but it already feels as though I've left that part of my life behind. I needed to. I only see Juliet once a month now, but when I do, she tells me that separating from my old life was probably the best thing I could've done.

On cue, Kane jogs down the stairs. He's wearing swim trunks and an Under Armor shirt and has a beach towel stuffed under his arm. He puts his sunglasses on and snaps at me. "Hey. You here to babysit the Pooper?"

I nod, as Mrs. Weeks gives him a look. "What did I tell you about—"

"I know, I know," he says, muttering under his breath, "Even though the kid is a poop machine. Catch you."

He leaves, and Mrs. Weeks shakes her head. "Like he's ever changed a diaper. So"—she looks around—"now that he's out of the way, I wonder if you could help me with a job."

I nod.

She brings me upstairs into Kane's disaster of a room. "Yesterday I found ants in here. Crawling up the baseboard," she says, shuddering. "He throws things around, and I don't think it's been thoroughly cleaned in years."

I clench my teeth. "You want me to clean Kane's room? Won't he be upset about that?"

She shakes her head. "I don't want you to clean. I want you to indiscriminately throw out stuff in there. I've warned him to do it on his own. This is war."

She slides open his closet, and I stare in horror. There are no clothes hung in there. It's like a Jenga tower of assorted belongings, all crammed in tightly. If it wasn't all so tightly jammed in there, we'd be buried under an avalanche. "Oh my."

"Just toss it. Toss it all."

"Even the—"

"All of it."

I stare at her. Going through Kane's private things seems like snooping through a diary. And throwing it all out? I have to remember that Kane was never one to be sentimental. He keeps stuff for one reason only: he's a slob. He'll probably be glad if I help him to clean his closet.

She gives me a roll of heavy-duty garbage bags, and I get to work. I throw away more recent junk, like the crown he got as prom king, the cheap, gilded aluminum bent beyond recognition. I look in a shoebox and toss the flowers he got for Valentine's Day, all of them nothing more than brown, shriveled petals. The cover had been on so securely that I don't think he looked at the messages again after that day.

By afternoon, I'm finding stuff that probably hasn't seen the light of day since elementary school—vocabulary books, a cracked Frisbee from a restaurant that closed down ten years ago, a leash for Mimsy, the dog he had that ran away when we were in kindergarten. I have to hold my nose to keep from gagging, because the closet smells a little like Kane, but mostly like body odor and rot.

Sitting back, I stretch and massage my aching back, surveying my progress. My stomach is growling. I've spent hours on this and have three giant bags of garbage, but looking at the closet, I've barely made a dent. And what's that thing on the floor? An ancient, calcified cheese stick? Gross.

As I lean forward to dig in again, Mrs. Weeks comes by, balancing baby Cooper on her hip. "Wow," she says. "I'm surprised you haven't uncovered the lost city of Atlantis yet."

"There's still time," I mumble.

"Well, I have lunch on the table," she says. "Grilled cheese and tomato soup. Come down and take a break."

"Thanks. I will in a minute," I tell her, wiping my hands on my shirt.

She leaves to feed the baby. I'm about to follow her downstairs when I notice a glistening gold statue, hidden underneath an old papier-mâché art project. I lift it out, wondering how it could've gotten in there. It's a baseball trophy, the biggest one he has, the one he got from regionals two years ago. When I yank it free of all the other junk, the base is bent. No, not bent. It's broken.

Nothing a little wood glue wouldn't fix. I sigh. Kane was probably too lazy to do even that, which is why it ended up where it was. I start to set it aside, thinking that of all the junk in this closet, that's one thing he definitely wouldn't want me to throw away.

Then I notice the corner of the broken base is crusted with dried blood.

The Day Of

I hadn't slept that night, but it didn't matter.

It was Valentine's Day, and I was in love. The world seemed brighter as I drove to school. The dreary mid-February day threatened snow, but I felt as if I was bathed in brilliant sunshine.

When I walked into homeroom, I saw the box of flowers—red and white carnations—on the teacher's desk. One of those, I knew, was for me. I watched the teacher drone on with the morning announcements. I was so excited, my skin buzzed. She talked about the likelihood that we'd have our first early dismissal of the year, since the snow was supposed to arrive before lunch. She said that if so, we'd have to come back to homeroom for dismissal, to avoid chaos.

Come on, come on, I thought, tapping my fingers on my desk.

Then she asked one of the Key Clubbers to distribute the flowers. The student did so, moving too slowly. Seconds ticked by. A couple times, he came near me, and I expected a flower to land on my desk. But one never did. When the bell ending the period rang, he dropped the empty box in the trash can at the front of the classroom.

I frowned. Then I looked at my phone. There was a message from Javier.

Schuyler wants to know where Declan is. Do you know?

Mrs. Schuyler was Declan's first-period physics teacher.

He wasn't in class?

No. And he had an exam today.

Did you text him?

Yeah. No response.

I opened a text to Declan.

Hey. Where are you?

I waited a few moments as I gathered my things to get to my second-period class, English, but when I looked at my phone, he still hadn't responded. The message said Delivered but hadn't switched to Read. I frowned and typed one to Kane: **Hey, have you seen Declan?**

A moment later, the text came back: No

He's not at school. Have you seen him?

No

He was up late last night. You think he overslept?

Are you kidding?

Yeah, it was a dumb idea. Declan once said he had an internal alarm clock that always, whether he wanted it to or not, woke him up at five in the morning. He was an early bird, for sure, which was why he was always taking the first bus into school.

Maybe he's sick. The flu's going around. Did you see him at home?

No

Great. It was as if Kane was being deliberately unhelpful with his short texts. I gave up.

In the hallway, people were flaunting their flowers like badges of honor. I thought I'd run into Kane there, as we usually crossed paths between homeroom and second period, while he was on his way to his level two English class, which was next to my Spanish class. But I didn't see him. I frowned as I walked into English and saw a small collection of unclaimed flowers on the desk. I looked through them, wondering if mine had gotten lost in the wrong homeroom. But they were all for Kane, from various girls.

Where was Kane? And why did Declan not give me a flower?

Then I sat down for the world's most mind-numbing lecture on *conjugación en pretérito*. Meanwhile, I kept sneaking looks at my phone under my desk, hoping Declan would reply.

But he didn't even read the message.

When I drove home early that afternoon, around lunchtime, I thought I'd be a good girlfriend and bring him chicken soup.

Not homemade, strictly Campbell's, but knowing Declan, he'd appreciate it. There was no snow yet, just a bit of a weird, spritzy fog. When I pulled into the driveway, I looked at his window. The blinds were closed. He was probably on death's door in there. I went inside, then cursed when I opened our pantry and realized we didn't have any soup at all.

When I next looked outside, it had started to snow.

That was when I heard a loud, mournful wail.

Monday, July 8
EVENING

By the time Kane returns home, it's dark. I'd helped Mrs. Weeks take all the bags of garbage to the curb. I'd hid the trophy in my backpack, then smuggled it into my room. When he pulls up at his house, I'm waiting for him. I push open my window and scream his name as he gets out of his car.

He turns to me and starts to jog over. He stops at the driveway, and maybe he can see me trembling, because he says, "What? What happened?"

I go downstairs and let him in, then take him upstairs to my room. Kane has a sunburn that's threatening to become a tan on his cheeks, and he smells like sunshine and seawater. He keeps asking me what the problem is, but I don't speak until I've closed the door and locked it. "Declan…"

I can't say anymore. A thousand thoughts are going through

my mind, but nothing comes out. I reach under my bed, pull out the trophy, and lay it on my bed.

His eyes widen. "Where did you get that?"

"In your bedroom." I stare at it, shaking uncontrollably. Every thought in my head has arrived at the same conclusion: This is the murder weapon that killed Declan. "Kane, what did you do?"

He holds out a hand. "You need to chill out."

"It's covered in blood, Kane! And it's all bashed in! Did you—"

"No. No!" he says, reaching over to grab me. I skirt away, around the bed, but he's too fast. He leaps over the bed and takes me by the shoulders. "Listen. I don't know why that's there."

"You're lying," I say. Of course he knows. Kane was proud of each and every one of his trophies. It had been missing from his dresser, and yet he hadn't said a thing about it. If it had suddenly disappeared, he would've wanted to know what had happened to it. "It's his blood, isn't it?"

He stares at me for a full ten seconds before he nods. He closes his eyes.

"Tell me."

He takes a deep breath. "I never went to school that Valentine's Day. Our parents were away, so I'd stayed up late the night before, watching sports on television, and I'd fallen asleep on the couch. I woke up late and went upstairs to get ready for school, and I nearly fucking tripped on him."

My breath hitches.

"He was dead. Just lying there in the hallway. He'd been hit in the head with the trophy, and I saw the blood." He collapses suddenly, falling down on the bed, hunching over and burying his head in his arms.

My mouth opens, trying to form words. I can't believe what I'm hearing. After all this…it was true? "He was murdered?"

His head bobs a yes. He speaks to the floor, his voice muffled by his arms. "And all I could think was that the last time I'd seen you, you were so upset. You told me you couldn't live like that, apart from Declan."

"But I…"

"So I hid the trophy. I was going to put it in his room, but I'd grown up in this house and didn't want…so I dragged him out to the shed. I…I didn't know what to do. I…" He takes in a shaky breath, then lets it out slowly. "I found my father's gun. I propped him up in there. I made it look like a suicide."

"My God," I breathe out, covering my mouth with my hands. "You shot him?"

"He was already dead," Kane says, his voice trembling. "You have to believe that he was already dead."

"But why?" I shout at him, no longer able to stand on my own. I sink onto the bed next to him, stunned. "If he was murdered, why would you do that?"

THAT NIGHT

He looks at me, and there are tears in his eyes. "Why do you think? Goddamn it, Hailey, everything I've ever done is to protect you."

The Day After

The Weeks family was already talking funeral plans. He'd been dead one day, and they were at the funeral parlor, making arrangements.

All I could think was that he wasn't dead. It was a mistake.

I got a thousand calls and texts from people. Each one of them was someone asking whether I needed help. But I didn't need help. I didn't need anyone anymore. I kept thinking, *This is a mistake. We're forever. We're forever. We're forever.*

That afternoon, I climbed the trellis to Declan's room. The window was locked, so I climbed down and found the key that Kane kept in a sad pot of dirt that used to have flowers. I opened the door, climbed the stairs, and cried on his bed. I inhaled the woodworker's glue and the motor oil. I thought about the last time we'd been together. I thought about lying in the dirty snow, in the pirate ship, staring up at the stars. I thought of his heart, beating so fiercely under my ear. Forever had been tainted; now it was a death sentence.

When Kane appeared, I didn't even stir. He just stood in the doorway, and though I could feel his presence, I ignored it. I wanted to lie in this room forever, maybe even die here. Nothing else mattered.

Finally, he said my name. I was surprised at how strong his voice was. I looked up. His eyes were rimmed darkly, probably from lack of sleep, as if something had finally chinked the great Kane Weeks's armor.

Very calmly, he asked me, "What did you do?"

"What do you mean?" I asked him, burying my face again.

"You know."

"No, I don't." My phone buzzed. I looked at it. Another text from another "concerned friend" who'd barely ever texted me before. "Why do people keep texting me?"

Without thinking, I threw my phone, as hard as I could. It hit the wall and shattered instantly, the pieces showering one of Declan's prized models of the *Titanic*.

Kane grabbed me by the shoulders, holding me still as my whole body heaved. He stood so close that I couldn't open my eyes without seeing him. As much as I didn't want to, he caught my gaze and held it. "Hailey. What did you do?"

I started to sob. "I think I made a mistake."

He nodded. "You think?"

Then I focused on him. "What did *you* do?"

"What I always do. What I will *always* do." He released me as if I was worthless, and I pushed away from him. I ran home across the street, wanting so badly to follow Declan, wherever he'd gone.

Monday, July 8

LATE

He's staring at me like he's waiting for me to admit something.

And I won't. I won't do it. Not now. Not after everything I've lost. I've lost so much more than anyone else. I don't deserve the responsibility for this.

"Kane," I say. "How can you think I would do something like that?"

He closes his eyes, then opens them, as if he's having trouble believing this isn't a dream. "What?"

"You don't understand. After I spoke with you...Declan came to my house. He told me he'd made a mistake. He told me he wanted to be with me. And we kissed, and he..." I heave a sob. "He went home. And I was so happy."

He stares at me. When he speaks, his voice quavers. "I don't..."

"I loved him, Kane. I've never loved anyone like I loved him. I could never do that." I catch his eyes. "Were you…were you trying to be my Gatsby? Protecting me, the way he protected Daisy?"

He's beyond confused now. About the book, about what I'm telling him. All this time, he'd believed it was me. That I'd killed Declan. "Yeah." His eyes trail to the ground. "But I thought…"

"When he left, he told me that Luisa was coming over, and he planned to end things with her."

He blinks. "Luisa?"

I nod. "She did this. My God. She killed him."

Kane is still standing there, like a statue. As if he can't get it through his head. But it all makes complete sense to me. Emotion is bubbling in my heart, and something I'd said a long time ago. *I'll prove it, if it's the last thing I do. She'll see.*

I grab hold of the trophy and take a step toward the door.

Kane stands. His face is stricken with alarm, eyes wide and wild. "Wait. What are you doing?"

"We have to tell someone. Nina's dad. She can't be allowed to—"

He crosses the room in three strides and grabs the trophy. "No. Hold on. You can't do that, because… I mean, it's been a year. More than a year." His mouth moves, but nothing comes out for a moment, as if he's tallying the implications of this in his head. "And hell, Hailey. If you tell them, I'm going to get screwed. Wouldn't I be an accessory, because I covered it up?"

"But we can't just let it go!" I shout, horrified at the suggestion. "She needs to pay. She killed him, Kane."

He takes the trophy and sets it down. "Hailey. Can we please sleep on this?"

"You think I can get any sleep now?"

"Please," he says, clamping his hand over my arm, so hard and desperate that I couldn't move if I wanted to. "Tomorrow. I'll go with you tomorrow, if you want. Think of what Declan would do."

Declan? I have no doubt. He'd wait. He always did things so carefully. So thoughtfully. Reluctantly, I nod.

But I will not let Luisa get away with this. She took Declan from me, more than once. And she needs to pay.

Three Days After

The funeral was something else.

Thousands of people packed into the funeral home for the memorial and drove in the procession to the cemetery. The priest remarked more than once that he'd never seen such an outpouring of love and support.

Kane went with his family at the front of the procession. I was stuck in the back, with Nina and Javier. Nina had been crying nonstop since she'd heard the news. Javier was driving, reaching out every so often to pull her close, kissing her forehead. For the first time, it struck me that Javier hadn't been forced with Nina because of all of us. From the way he kept holding her, touching her, looking at her to make sure she was okay, he really cared.

Declan once cared about me like that.

Now he was dead. About to be put in the ground for eternity.

I fingered the necklace I'd taken to wearing—even when I

slept and showered—and swallowed a sob. *Diamonds are forever. And so are we.*

Because Javier's SUV was at the end of the procession and rain was coming down in ceaseless sheets, by the time we'd slogged over the muddy patches of snow to the grave site, the ceremony had already begun. I had to stand behind rows and rows of people, and I couldn't hear the priest over the patter of rain and the sobs of onlookers.

Not a single one of us had an umbrella. I'm not sure if it was because the rain hadn't been forecast, or because we'd all been too aggrieved to think of it. But I stood there, in the mud, thinking that rain always falls on the funerals of the truly virtuous. *Blessed are the dead that the rain falls on.*

Afterward, we were all able to walk past the grave and throw a flower onto the coffin after it was lowered into the ground. I waited for what seemed like hours for my turn, my puffer coat and navy-blue dress so soaked that I could feel rainwater sliding down my rib cage. My hair was as wet as if I'd emerged from the shower without wringing it out. Trailing behind Nina and Javier, I took one of the last roses from the bucket, and as I did, my eyes met those of Mr. and Mrs. Weeks, Kane, and Luisa.

Luisa stared at me as I looked over the casket, trying to think of words I could say to Declan. The only thing that came wasn't very eloquent, but I suppose it said it all. *I'm sorry.*

Before I could throw in my rose, someone snatched my wrist. "He doesn't need anything from you," Luisa snapped at me.

I lost my grip on the flower, and it tumbled into the mud by my soaked boots. I stared at her, wondering whether those were tears or raindrops on her face.

"He never loved you," she whispered in my ear. "And with good reason. He told me everything you did to him. You don't need to be here. So just go."

I didn't pick up the flower. I pulled away and walked back to Javier's car. She couldn't be right. He did love me. He *had* loved me. If there hadn't been a Luisa, he'd still be alive. *She* was the one who'd ruined it all.

Back in Javier's SUV, he and Nina tried to talk to me, about what a lovely ceremony it had been, but I wasn't listening.

"He loved me. And I'll prove it, if it's the last thing I do," I said to no one in particular as I stared out the rain-streaked window. "She'll see."

Tuesday, July 9

That morning, bright and early, I get into my Jeep, with Kane at my side.

We have someplace to be.

We need to set this to rest. And once this is done, we can finally move on.

I'm carrying my backpack with the evidence. A night of sleep only made me surer that Luisa needs to suffer. She doesn't deserve to go off to college and live her life after she ended Declan's. After she ended mine.

Kane looks unnaturally pale. He says to me, his voice soft, "Hailey."

I look at him as I rev the engine. Yes, he's nervous. He's worried about what will happen to him when they find out he covered up Declan's murder. "What?"

"What about the box of his things?" he says softly. "Don't you need that?"

He's stalling. But I'll give him that. Part of me hopes he's starting to understand my viewpoint and is on my side with this. She may be his girlfriend, but right is right. I don't think anything in that box is more damning than the statue, but I suppose it makes sense to bring it with us, to give the police a full picture of what was happening before Declan died. I open the door. "If you think so."

I jog out into the warm summer air and into the house. I'd thought about tossing the box a thousand times, but it's still under my bed, where I stashed it after that day during the winter when I'd gone through it. I pull it out and hurry downstairs.

But when I get to the car, my skin prickles.

The car is still running, and the passenger seat is empty.

I look toward the Weeks house, hoping that maybe Kane simply went home to get something, but when I peer inside the Jeep, my backpack is missing.

My heart jams in my throat. The evidence.

I whirl around, and my eyes fasten on a form moving through the trees at the end of the cul-de-sac. With a sinking feeling, I know where Kane is headed.

I tear off after him, screaming his name. "Kane, don—" I shout as I enter the clearing, seeing him crouching over the fire pit with the backpack, a container of lighter fluid, and a lighter.

"Let us go, Hailey," he says softly in a quiet but commanding voice. I thought I knew every side of Kane, but I've never seen this one, and it's why my shout dies in my throat. He looks up at me as he finds a flame and touches the lit tip to the canvas fabric. "Please."

I've never heard his voice so fragile. He's begging me. I can do nothing but stare helplessly as the bag starts to smolder, then bursts into flames.

Everything I know might as well be burning with it.

He comes beside me, reaches into his pocket, unfolds a piece of paper, and stares at it. Then he hands it to me. "I found this in his room the day he died."

I glance at it, then look away. I know what it is. It's a note to accompany my Valentine's Day flower. It says:

You're the most amazing person I know.—Declan

The tears hit my cheeks even before I see that it's not written out to me. It's written out to Luisa.

"Why would he have written this if he was breaking up with Luisa?"

"He didn't hand it in," I protest.

"But he still wrote it. To her."

I swallow. I shrug. I tug on the hem of my shorts with both hands.

"Hailey," Kane says. "You have to let us go. It. Ends. Here. Do you understand? For me. For Declan. It ends here and now."

I bring my hands to my face and cover it, hoping to shield myself from him. "No."

"Yes, Hailey. It's over."

I swallow as he looks back at the flames, now consuming the entire backpack. He throws Declan's note into the fire, and then sinks to his knees. "Oh God, Hailey. God. You know, when I thought about going to college, the thousands of choices out there, I thought, in four years, I could be one of a thousand different people. It all depended on what choice I made from here." He shakes his head and looks up at the smoke, climbing into the trees. "And then I thought, *Or I can stay here. With what's comfortable.* And part of me kept wanting to tread that safe, narrow road."

I look at him. He falls back onto his backside, throwing his arms over his bended knees.

"But we can't. We have to move on. And when I saw what you had done, I knew we couldn't stay on that road."

Tears fall faster now, but I wipe them away. "He was supposed to be with me. He was *meant* to be with me. And she's the reason he's dead. It's her."

He shakes his head. "Maybe she's a part of it. But she didn't know what would happen. You can't do this."

"I...I was so angry at him for leaving me. I couldn't stand it. I know I wasn't the best girlfriend in the world, but how could he leave me?"

He shakes his head. "I know why you wanted to hurt her. But this isn't right. You know that. She may be a pain in the ass, but she doesn't deserve that."

I sniff. "She gets everything. And I have nothing. I don't even have you."

"You really think that Luisa and I are going to last?" he asks with an ironic laugh. I look at him. "We can't go back. Every time we get back together, something is lost. I think by Christmas, we'll both be seeing other people. But you'll always have me, Hailey. All right?"

No. Nothing is all right. I think about that night. I'd sneaked up the trellis in the cold, but I could hear Luisa's high-pitched voice, even from outside, even with the window closed. I scaled the peak of the roof, then went into Kane's window, hoping I could cry to him.

But he hadn't been there. Instead, I'd sat on his bed, feeling so alone.

It's that loneliness that creeps over me now, threatening to crush me. I remember looking up at the trophies as I listened to the sound of them laughing together in the next room over.

I stared at Kane's never-vacuumed blue carpeting for an eternity, waiting. I imagined Luisa's sweet, angelic smile, brightening Declan's mood in the way only I was supposed to be capable of. I remember the door opening, and the light spilling into the hallway.

And then I had my hand on the trophy.

I ripped it from the dresser. I stormed into the darkened hallway, wanting to beat that smug, candy-coated smile off her face.

I brought it down once, with calculated, silent force.

That was all it took. I raised it over my head again, but I didn't need to.

The figure staggered backward without a sound, hitting the wooden flooring in the hallway, motionless before I could swing it again.

Good, I'd thought. *Maybe that'll smack some sense into her. Or permanently disfigure her.*

I waited for Declan to come out of his room and see how much I loved him. He'd see how lost I was without him, and he'd save me from this hell I was living.

But he didn't.

Two seconds later, common sense trickled in, replacing the rage that had been boiling inside me, and a second after that, it morphed into fear. My fingers loosened on the trophy, and I studied it, surprised to see it in my hands. What the hell had I done?

When I crept closer, I realized my mistake. The form on the floor wasn't Luisa. No, she'd left through the window.

Declan was lying at my feet.

Motionless.

The skull near his forehead, just above that arched eyebrow, was bleeding. Dented unnaturally.

I said his name. Once. Twice.

No answer. I dropped the trophy.

I ran, nearly diving out his window, slipping on the snow on the roof, falling to the bushes without feeling a thing.

I did this. I built these walls. The reason I've been in hell for so long? I belong there. And Kane can't save me from it. Not when the devil's saved a seat for me.

I can try to move forward, make my life as worthy and meaningful as two to compensate for the one I took. But Declan was a star, bound for greatness, and try though I might, nothing I do will ever be as magnificent as what he would've done. In one second of madness, I destroyed it all. And that will be with me for the rest of my life, touching every little thing I do.

I'd wanted something to make me special. And now I have it. I'm a murderer.

"When I saw him there, I thought about what Declan would want," Kane says. "And I knew he'd want me to take care of you. To fall on the sword on your behalf. To be your Gatsby."

I look at him. "You...finished the book?"

"Yeah. Fucking Gatsby." He lets out a long, heavy sigh. "I did a really shitty thing to protect you, Hailey, and now Declan will always be known as the kid who committed suicide. He loved you, Hailey. More than anyone, even him, could possibly put into words, so I have to believe he would've wanted me to do that. But maybe he understood then what I'm only now realizing.

"You're the first. And you may be the most intense. I may never feel the things I felt for you again. But even the smallest action can bend us in ways so that we don't go back. You did it to him when you kept us a secret from him. And you did it to me too."

"But—" I shudder, the full weight of his words bearing down on me. Of course, I know what he's talking about.

"You knew what I did, and that it was for you. And did you care? No, you were still willing to throw me away like garbage, to send me to jail, to get your revenge on Luisa."

I open my mouth to explain, but he doesn't want that.

"Hailey. Stop. It doesn't matter." His voice is hard. "What I'm saying is, you can't be the last."

I stare at the flames. With those five words, my life might as well be over. Deep inside, I think I always thought I'd eventually end up with one of them. My life, so entwined with the Weeks boys… Does he understand what he's saying? How can I go on living without my heart?

But I suppose this is what I deserve, so I say nothing.

"I'm not going to end up facedown in a pool with a bullet in my back, Hailey," he says. "I'm luckier than him. I can move on from here, be one of the people I imagined. You have to let me. Say it's okay, and let me."

I can't speak. He wants permission, two words: *It's okay*. But those are not so easy to give. For so long, my life has been all about the Weeks boys. And he's right. Luisa's right. I've been a poison to them. And even if Declan can't go on from here because of me, at least there's something I can do for Kane.

I fall to my knees beside him, lost in tears. "I'm so sorry," I repeat, over and over again. "I'm so sorry."

He takes me in his arms and whispers in my ear, nothing I can make sense of. I'm not sure anything will ever make sense to me again. After all, I never knew it was possible to love someone to death, to hold him to your heart so tightly that he's crushed in your embrace.

But I have. And as long as I live, I will never do that again.

I nod. *It's okay*, I mouth. *It's okay*. I repeat it over and over, until it's more for myself than it is for him.

Kane closes his eyes, then wipes at one. Is he crying? By the time I can focus on him, they're dry, and he's back to the unemotional, unsentimental Kane I know and love.

"Kane," I say as I watch embers climb into the summer sky. "I wish we could go back."

He climbs to his feet and digs his hands into the pockets of his shorts. "I know."

After that, he takes my hand and we walk back to our houses. Standing toe to toe, I look up at him as he gently takes my face in his hands and wipes my tears with the pad of his thumb. He tells me that he will always love me, that I need to take care of myself, that I need to move on. *Move on, move on, move on. No going back. Ever forward, even when we're standing still.*

I will keep on this path, though I am falling, falling, falling through the endless hell I built around me. I may go to college and meet someone else, but I will never love that person with all of myself, the way I did the Weeks boys. I know that.

There will always be a part of me that belongs to them.

Now

I've started college, and my grades aren't terrible. Silas and I are dating, and life is okay on that front. I think I might even care about him, though not too much. Don't worry; I constantly keep that in check.

I'm moving on.

As humans, it's not possible to stay in one spot. The world moves around us, and we must move with it. And you would want me to, right, Declan?

Maybe I will find a place here, one day. But it will be a darker place, nothing like the one I imagined all those years ago, when you loved me.

But what is it they say? Shadows make one appreciate the light.

In my mind, our last night went like this: Under the starry sky, in the backyard, you told me that you still loved me, would always love me, and we had all the time in the world to be together. Our path stretched out before us like a long, winding, beautiful road.

But in reality? I suppose reality was much different.

I am my past. I can't escape it, and I can't lie down and die in it, so I'll carry it with me, in chains around me, for the rest of my life. I'll make myself as comfortable as I can, no matter how much the truth burdens me, and maybe one day you can forgive me.

I will never be the person you once believed I was.

But that hopeless romantic in me endures, a boat beating against the current. And I still believe in us.

Even if I'm the only one, Declan. I still believe in us.

Acknowledgments

My deepest appreciation to Annette and the whole wonderful team at Sourcebooks, my superb agent, Mandy, my amazing readers, and all of my family and friends who get me through each day, especially Sara, Gabrielle, and Brian. Thank you for everything.

About the Author

Cyn Balog is the author of a number of young adult novels. She lives outside Allentown, Pennsylvania, with her husband and daughters. Visit her online at cynbalog.com.

"A compelling, dark confessional with pages that keep you guessing and an ending that will blow you sideways."

—NATALIE RICHARDS, author of *Six Months Later* and *One Was Last* on *Unnatural Deeds*

ALONE

CYN BALOG

You're Never Really Alone

1
-

Welcome to the Bismarck-Chisholm House—
where murder is only the beginning of the fun!
Stay in one of our eighteen comfortable guest rooms.
You'll sleep like the dead. We guarantee it...

Sometimes I dream I am drowning.

Sometimes I dream of bloated faces, bobbing on the surface of misty waters.

And then I wake up, often screaming, heart racing, hands clenching fistfuls of my sheets.

I'm in my bed at the top of Bug House. The murky daylight casts dull prisms from my snow globes onto the attic floor. My mom started collecting those pretty winter scenes for me when I was a baby. I gaze at them, lined neatly on the shelf in front of my window. My first order of business every day is hoping they'll give me a trace of the joy they did when I was a kid.

But either they don't work that way anymore, or I don't.

Who am I kidding? It's definitely me.

I'm insane. Batshit. Nuttier than a fruitcake. Of course, that's not an official diagnosis. The official word from Dr. Batton, whose swank Copley Square office I visited only once when I was ten, was that I was bright and intelligent and a *wonderful young person*. He said it's normal for kids to have imaginary playmates.

But it gets a little sketchy when that young person grows up, and her imaginary friend decides to move in and make himself comfortable.

Not that anyone knows about that. No, these days, I'm good about keeping up appearances.

My second order of business each day is hoping that *he* won't leak into my head. That maybe I can go back to being a normal sixteen-year-old girl.

But he always comes.

He's a part of me, after all. And he's been coming more and more, invading my thoughts. *Of course I'm here, stupid.*

Sawyer. His voice in my mind is so loud that it drowns out the moaning and creaking of the walls around me.

"Seda, honey?" my mother calls cheerily. She shifts her weight on the bottom step, making the house creak more. "Up and at 'em, buckaroo!"

I force my brother's taunts away and call down the spiral staircase, "I *am* up." My short temper is because of him, but it ends up directed at her.

She doesn't notice though. My mother has only one mood now: ecstatically happy. She says it's the air up here, which always has her taking big, deep, monster breaths as if she's trying to inhale the entire world into her lungs. But maybe it's because this is her element; after all, she made a profession out of her love for all things horror. Or maybe she really is better off without my dad, as she always claims she is.

I hear her whistling "My Darlin' Clementine" as her slippered feet happily scuffle off toward the kitchen. I put on the first clothing I find in my drawer—sweatpants and my mom's old Boston College sweatshirt—then scrape my hair into a ponytail on the top of my head as I look around the room. Mannequin body parts and other macabre props are stored up here. It's been my bedroom for only a month. I slept in the nursery with the A and Z twins when we first got here because they were afraid of ghosts and our creepy old house. But maybe they—like Mom—are getting used to this place?

The thought makes me shudder. I like my attic room because of the privacy. Plus, it's the only room that isn't ice cold, since all the heat rises up to me. But I don't like much else about this old prison of a mansion.

One of the props, Silly Sally, is sitting in the rocker by the door as I leave. She'd be perfect for the ladies' department at Macy's if it weren't for the gaping chest wound in her frilly pink blouse. "I hate you," I tell her, batting at the other mannequin body parts descending from the rafters like some odd canopy. She smiles as if the feeling is mutual. I give her a kick on the way out.

Despite the morbid stories about this place, I don't ever worry about ghosts. After all, I have Sawyer, and he is worse.

As I climb down the stairs, listening to the kids chattering in the nursery, I notice the money, accompanied by a slip of paper, on the banister's square newel post. The car keys sit atop the pile. Before I can ask, Mom calls, "I need you to go to the store for us. OK, Seda, my little kumquat?"

I blink, startled, and it's not because of the stupid nickname. I don't have a license, just a learner's permit. My mom had me driving all over the place when we first came here, but that was *back then*. Back when this was a simple two-week jaunt to get an old house she'd inherited ready for sale. There wasn't another car in sight, so she figured, why not? She's all about giving us kids *experiences*, about making sure we aren't slaves to our iPhones, like so many of my friends back home. My mother's always marching to her own drummer, general consensus be damned, usually to my horror. But back then, I had that thrilling, invincible, first-days-of-summer-vacation feeling that made anything seemed possible. Too bad that was short lived.

We've been nestled at Bug House like hermits for months. Well, that's not totally true. Mom has made weekly trips down the mountain, alone, to get the mail and a gallon of milk and make phone calls to civilization. We were supposed to go back to Boston before school started, but that time came and went, and there's no way we're getting off this mountain before the first snow.

Snow.

I peer out the window. The first dainty flakes are falling from the sky.

Snow. Oh God. Snow.

My mother appears in the doorway, her body drowning out most of the morning light from the windows behind her. She'd never be considered fat, but *substantial,* tall and striking. Mom is someone people intrinsically want to imitate. She was one of the most popular professors last year at Boston College. My father used to say all the young men in her lectures were in love with her, and all the young women wanted to be like her. She can make a glamorous entrance even when stepping out of her car to get gas. That—and her size—are what separate us, people say. I'm short and rail thin, and people don't usually pay attention to what I say or do.

"Why the sourpuss?" Mom says airily, twirling her blond curls into an elegant chignon at the base of her neck. "Is it because we're not going back just yet?"

I don't know how to respond. She says *just yet,* but I hear *ever.* The snow only cements the word in my head. My mother loves changing plans. She doesn't let other people's schedules dictate what we should do, which is why I've always missed lots of school. My mother will get these crazy ideas for adventure, like crabbing in the bay or going off to Old Sturbridge Village for a candle-making seminar, and we pick up and go. Like I said, life experience. *Books and the inside of a classroom can only teach you so much,* she says. It's part of why her students love her.

"It's only a little longer, all right?" she says, surveying the foyer in a lovestruck way. "We're very close to having a buyer for the house."

She's told me that before, but plans have changed a dozen times since June. I hate to think of what will happen if they change any more. *Fun* is what my friends used to call my mother. Except that brand of "fun" can wear you down.

"But..." I trail off, a million buts dying on my lips. But *everything.* It's one thing to live in such a remote place during the summer, when the surrounding landscape is bursting with color and the birds are singing. But in the winter?

What are you complaining about? Sawyer asks me. *People like you shouldn't be part of the general public.*

And maybe it's true. Maybe being alone with my family on the side of a mountain will keep everyone from finding out what is going on inside my head. That *he* is there, always threatening to take over. Maybe, without the outside world to intrude, Dr. Maya Helm's crazy daughter can just go on being crazy.

Not that I can tell my mother that. No, to her, Sawyer was my fictitious childhood playmate who has long been forgotten.

But the thing is, Sawyer had been coming to me more and more since we came here. He's always in the back of my head, that little voice spurring me to be a little wild whenever I want to hold back and play it safe. At first, I thought everyone had a Sawyer, like when he told me to throw a binder at Lucy Willis for calling me ugly in third grade or touch a hot radiator when I was two. Gradually though, I learned Sawyer's voice was something to keep quiet. Still, back home in Boston, I had distractions to drown him out. I had studies and color guard and friends.

Here, he is front and center in my thoughts, twenty-four seven.

And Sawyer likes it this way. Even though my head is screaming that we need to get as far away from this place as possible, one part of me, the part of my stomach that's supposed to get queasy and unsettled, feels warm. Comfortable.

My mother comes up to me and swipes a stray lock of hair from my face. I flinch. "Don't."

"Everything's OK, love." She gives me a convincing smile, even though the world might as well be crumbling around us. "I know you're bored to death here, but I promise, we'll be back home soon."

I *wish* it was just boredom. I swallow and nod, then slide the money and keys in the pocket of my sweatshirt and head out the door before the kids can notice me. If this weather continues, I can't delay. The mountain road we live on is no joke. Our van nearly slid into a ditch during a light rain, so snow won't be any better. Not that I've ever been here in the winter.

The van creaks to life, and I pull out of the decaying three-bay garage and down the winding driveway, pinging gravel into the air behind the car. The snow looks almost pretty, landing delicately on the windshield.

It's twenty miles to Art's General, the closest store. I listen to the radio part of the way, but the only station we get is all static-filled talk about the blizzard that's coming. Twenty inches expected, at least. I switch off the radio and try to ignore the tension in my hands from gripping the steering wheel so tightly. I concentrate on the tree-lined road. Of course I'd noticed the days getting darker and colder, but I thought it was only September. I'm losing track of time now, ever since Dad checked out in the middle of the night without so much as a goodbye.

August 31. Three days before the official start of school. That was the last I saw him. The details are hazy, like a dream. Sawyer sees to that. But the outcome is the same. Dad's gone. And we are alone with Mom and her whims.

This early in the morning, the parking lot at Art's is empty.

Not that it's ever crowded. When I lived in Boston, weather like this packed the stores with frantic people stocking up on bread and milk and toilet paper. But there simply *are* no people to pack Art's. It's a wonder the store stays in business, but a good thing it does. Otherwise we'd probably starve to death.

I navigate around the old snowblower carcasses he has for sale on the sidewalk, then push open the heavy door. When the bell over the door tinkles, Elmer, who took over after Art died, stares at me like I'm a ghost. "Seda?"

I give him a wave.

He cranes his neck to look out the window. "Your mom with you?"

That's the most he's said to me, ever. Elmer's never been a talker, so if I go about my business, he should leave me alone. "Not today," I say, then turn to my list. It's a mile long and has things like hot cocoa and canned vegetables and bottled water on it.

Either she's way overestimating our appetites, or this is a *We're not going back to Boston* list.

I slump against the canned goods display, then startle at the horrifically loud crash as half a dozen tomato soup cans go scattering and rolling in all directions. Elmer just scowls and picks up his crossword puzzle. I fish after the cans and restack them quickly. As I'm piling items into a basket and trying to decide whether I should buy the kids SpaghettiOs as a treat, the bell dings again and I hear a sound that makes me freeze.

Laughter.